I0521399

Star-Struck

by Twyla Turner

©Copyright 2014 Twyla Turner

To my parents,
who have always believed that I am destined for
greatness. And for Sharon, who made me realize that life is too
short not to follow my dream. You are missed.

This is a work of fiction. Names, characters, businesses, places, events and incidents are either the products of the author's imagination or used in a fictitious manner. Any resemblance to actual persons, living or dead, or actual events is purely coincidental.

Table of Contents:

Chapter 1

Madison "Sunny" Stone believed in fairy tales. She knew it was silly, but always had. *Damn Cinderella and her freaking glass pumps!* She thought to herself. The iconic princess, her godmother, and her little disease infested rats had infused the whole 'love concurs all' belief deep into her psyche. As well as every other princess story, T.V. drama, romance novel and well placed fragrance ad she'd encountered throughout the years.

So as she sat chowing down on popcorn, with an empty pint of *Ben & Jerry's Chocolate Chip Cookie Dough* next to her, chugging a big boy can of *Coors Light*, while having a mini-movie marathon that consisted of *Tangled*, *The Notebook* and Gabriel Wolf's new romantic movie Estranged; Sunny realized that old habits die hard. It was glaringly obvious, as she stared down at a soon-to-be 35 years past, that though fairy tales very well may happen to others, genetically pre-disposed to perfection, *us Plain Janes are fucked.*

Sunny's life seemed to play out like a romantic comedy, minus the romantic part. She hadn't been on a date in four years. Hadn't been asked out on any either, not unless she counted the lecherous old men that came into her work. Which she didn't. She couldn't even get a date through the online dating sites she had tried. Her inboxes, as well as her 'other' box, were decidedly empty.

The closest she had been to sex in the past four years was her trusty old friend the Rascally Rabbit. She had become proficient in the art of self-gratification. Well except for that one time when she passed out drunk while pleasuring herself. Only to awaken with her pants around her ankles legs spread wide with a very dead Rabbit sticking out of her hoo-ha! But besides that 'crawl in a whole and die' inducing moment, she had to be an expert masturbator, because even when she was in a relationship, no man had ever gotten her "there". Her entire life had about as much passion as a constipated man's first bowel movement.

She hit the pause button in frustration, of course freezing the screen at the most pivotal moment in *The Notebook*, the kiss in the rain. Rolling her eyes in frustration, she shuffled her slippered feet to the fridge for another beer. Passing the full-length mirror hanging on her bathroom door, her reflection caught her eye. Normally she avoided mirrors like the plague, building a bubble of semi-self-confidence around her. Always afraid of the disappointment there would be from looking too closely. But this time she really looked. She tried to look thoroughly and objectively. Trying to see what others, specifically men, might see.

A Mocha Latte with a touch of cream complexion. Pretty, medium sized honey brown almond shaped eyes, with a thick fringe of average length curling eyelashes. No medieval-eyelid-pinching-eyelash-curling-torture device needed. *Thank God for that!* A small button nose, high round cheekbones that got even higher and rounder when she smiled, which is how she got the nickname Sunny. As well as rashes as a child from people always wanting to pinch and kiss her cheeks.

Then there were her lips, her absolute favorite thing about her face. Which she could never understand why there weren't more guys lined up to kiss her senseless like Ryan Gosling did to Rachel McAdams. They were a perfect bow shape, full and soft and small. Like a bee stung baby doll as opposed to a Botox injected big mouth bass.

Sighing at the tragedy of her un-kissed lips, her eyes moved finally to her hair. A mass of long brown golden highlighted, (*ahhh makeover in a bottle*) tightly coiled corkscrew curls that sprang up in disarray all over her head and bounced lightly on her shoulders and back. She knew most men loved hair that they could put their fingers through, but not much was getting through her mess of curls. She shrugged, knowing it was what she had to work with. She was never going back to the financial and chemical torture of straightening her hair.

"Take me as is," she said to herself, shrugging as her eyes moved downward.

She felt her face could pass for pretty, maybe even beautiful on a good day. But that's where it stopped. Next up, was her body. So there were females that were called "butter-face", meaning "everything but-her face". She thought a "butter-body", sounded more appropriate when describing herself. Pretty face, kind, thoughtful with an outgoing personality. But looking down at her body in the full length mirror, all she felt was shame, made worse since moving to Southern California four years ago.

Standing at five-feet-two, the best term she could come up with was "round", or maybe "butterball". Large heavy breasts that looked great in a bra. But man, did gravity suck like a mother when it came off. And full upper arms with a decent helping of "Hello-Bettys". Translation: arms of an old lady flapping in the breeze when she waves to her friend Betty across the bingo hall, as she says "Hello Betty".

Then looking at her mid-section, lifting up her over-sized t-shirt to see better, was a soft rounded tummy with a hint of soon-to-be training wheel sized love handles (*Ha! No "love" here*), where there should be a sleek waistline. Turning slightly to see a decently rounded heart-shaped, if not slightly large behind. And attached to that were; wide hips, thick thighs and shapely but pretty calves. She felt her only saving grace was at least she was equally 'round' all over.

Through the years though she learned how to hide the negatives pretty well and accentuate the positives just as good. Dressing well was like a fine art to her. *I'm heavy, but I don't have to be dumpy and frumpy. Or worse....scandalous!* She'd learned that big baggy clothes just made her look bigger. But tighter clothes in the wrong places made her look a hot mess and that's when mothers are shielding their kids' eyes, before they can see her and start pointing. No, she knew she could dress her ass off for any occasion. She couldn't hide the fact that she was chubby, but most people thought she was smaller than what she actually was. It was just thinking about the clothes coming off in front of male eyes that made her quiver in fear.

Her cellphone rang bringing her out of her sad perusal of her appearance. Running to the fridge to grab a beer and back to her coffee table where her phone sat, she saw that it was her best friend Alyssa.

"Yellow," she answered, smiling into the phone.

"Hey, girlie! What are you doing?" Alyssa practically shouted in Sunny's ear.

Sunny cracked open her beer. "Oooh, not much."

"Madison Stone, are you drinking your three-pack of tall cans, watching sappy romantic movies and eating ice cream again!" Alyssa yelled into her ear.

"I have no idea what you're talking about." She loudly sipped her beer, letting the ice cold liquid quench her frustrations. *Damn, how does she know me so well!*

"I can hear you slurping, you know." Sunny could just imagine Alyssa with hands on hips, and tapping foot.

"I'm sure. And I'll have you know that in my lineup is the new Gabriel Wolf movie. That makes all forgiven. So is there a reason for you calling to rudely interrupt my pity party?"

"Harrumph, well I never! As tempting as the smokin' hot Mr. Wolf is, I was just being an awesome friend and calling to see if you wanted to come out with me tonight. Because I am the most amazing person you know and just being in my presence would brighten anyone's day."

Sunny shook her head in amazement. "Your self-esteem knows no bounds. But as honored as I am to be friends with such an incredible individual such as yourself, I am not feeling up to being social."

"Aw come on Sunny! Live up to the name! Shine some of your light on us drunken fools." Alyssa whined.

"I have to work tomorrow and you know I have a gig after that. And besides I'm already in my pajamas." She could already tell she'd lost this fight. She usually did, but she put up one anyway.

Next came Alyssa's closing argument. "You don't have to work until noon. And as long as you don't sing for us tonight, your voice should be fine tomorrow night. And besides, your voice always sounds a little sexier with that 'I was out drinking last night' rasp you get."

She did kind of have a point. "Fine. Give me thirty minutes." Sunny tried to sound exasperated, but failed as usual.

"Rad! I'll be down in twenty-five to make sure you don't flake on me."

Only in California do they still use the terms "rad" and "gnarly", that those of us in the Midwest gave up in the 80's.

"Great." Insert sarcastic voice. And since Alyssa lived only two floors above Sunny's studio, she knew there was no escape.

~~~

After graduating from college into a crappy economy, with a degree in Creative Writing, Sunny got whatever jobs she could get. Unfortunately all she could get were retail jobs. She had started freaking out when she turned thirty, with no career in sight and trudging through the few pitiful relationships she'd had. The last one was particularly painful and toxic and lasted four years. All that combined, plus wanting to see more of the world than Illinois, taking what little savings she had, Sunny ran off to SoCal. In the hopes that she could write some amazing screenplays and be the next Ben Affleck/Matt Damon walking up to the podium to accept her *Oscar*.

Instead of living the life, riding the *Oscar* train from the plethora of job offers knocking down her door, she moved two thousand miles for beautiful weather and another shitty retail job. The best part thus far was getting involved in singing in nightclubs and meeting some great friends. One of which Sunny was waiting for in her apartment, after she received an emergency call to come upstairs to Alyssa's place so Sunny could help her pick out shoes for her outfit. Neurotic friend, but great.

Sitting on Alyssa's bed Sunny watched her friend on her

hands and knees with her tight perfect apple bottom in the air digging through her closet for a pair of shoes.

"You know you look great wearing anything, right?" Sunny said to Alyssa's behind.

She turned to look at Sunny as if she had grown horns or something. "No I don't. Besides Sunny, you know that I have to look great because that bitch Stephanie is working with Brandon tonight."

Although Alyssa was gorgeous with a great tall and slender body, blonde hair and big green Bambi eyes with amazing eyelashes most can only buy at the drugstore, she was more insecure about her appearance than Sunny. Sunny had basically accepted her body years ago and had learned to find things to love about herself. She may not have been completely happy with everything about herself, but Sunny had become reasonably comfortable in her own skin. She rarely mentioned or beat herself up about her flaws. Earlier, being the exception or when she was naked in front of a man. *Since that's not happening anytime soon...I'm good.* As for Alyssa though, she was a product of the California 'perfection' that everyone there tried to achieve.

"Alyssa, you need to stop worrying about that girl. You're gorgeous and Brandon is totally into you. Who does he take out on dates?" Sunny asked raising one brow.

"Me. But still every time she works with him she's all over him." Alyssa frowned.

"That's just because she's a cock-blockin' twat-swattin' troll!" Sunny grumbled.

Alyssa fell over laughing in hysterics. "Sunny, I love you!" She wiped at the tears on her face. "But you're gonna mess up my makeup."

"Well let's get going before I change my mind and put my pajamas back on. Grab your brown boots. They look good with what you're wearing."

"Alright."

Alyssa pulled her calf-high boots over her skinny jeans that she paired with a pretty coral colored flowy tank top and a long necklace. And as always, Alyssa's makeup was perfection. She used the whole arsenal: foundation, eye-shadow, eyeliner, mascara, blush and finally a shimmery lip-gloss. But the finished product always looked flawless and natural. *How does she do that shit...every time?!*

Sunny had opted for her usual stretchy boot cut jeans. Her short curvy legs didn't get along well with the newer skinny jean trend. They were called "skinny" for God's sake and skinny was one adjective that Sunny had never heard to describe her. So regulating herself to her normal comfort jeans she paired them with her favorite lace trimmed, black and white baby-doll flannel tank top and a black lace-backed sweater shrug to cover up her "Hello Bettys". The tank was cut low enough to show a tasteful amount of cleavage without looking like a hoochie, and long enough to cover her soft tummy. And it had pockets! *Any top, skirt or dress with pockets was a must-have! Right?*

To accessorize her look she added her signature hoop earrings, circa 1960's cat-eye eyeliner and mascara to bring out her almond shaped eyes. No foundation, because she touched her face too much and would only end up getting brown all over her clothes. And black ballet flats. No heels for her. She felt like an elephant on toothpicks in heels! Plus, she was all about comfort and there was nothing comfortable about walking around looking like a baby giraffe. So with that they were out the door for their typical weeknight out.

~~~

Sunny loved downtown Long Beach the minute she saw it. It was perfect for her. Far enough away from L.A. where the rent was decent, but still only a forty-five-minute drive with little traffic. *Little traffic? Ha good luck with that!* Though, it still had big city appeal with tall buildings, restaurants, bars and shops. And it was diverse, like where she grew up. Black, White, Latino and Asian all together. The biggest appeal was the ocean and the harbor, where they were headed. Alyssa's soon to be boyfriend

Brandon worked as a bartender at Thirty-three Degrees. A bar that sat on the harbor with other restaurants and shops called *Shoreline Village*, which was perfect walking distance from their apartment. It had quickly become their favorite spot.

As soon as Sunny and Alyssa walked up to the open patio area their usual drinking crew cheered their greetings to them. They went around the tables giving hugs and hellos. Their bar friends all worked at the other restaurants in the Village. Thirty-three just so happened to be the spot that everyone went to when they got off work. Most times there would only be a few here and there. Though tonight looked like it was going to be one of those rare nights that everyone showed up for an after work drink or two or three. This equaled an awesome night and a long exhausting day tomorrow for Sunny.

Sunny and Alyssa slipped into the bar to grab their usual drinks and Alyssa's kiss from Brandon. Alyssa got her customary vodka cranberry and Sunny got her usual *Coors Light* in a pint glass.

Alyssa took her first sip and sighed. "Hey did you see that they're filming something in town today? If they're still filming tomorrow, you need to go over and harass them until someone reads one of your screenplays."

"No, I never left the apartment today. And since I have to work tomorrow, I don't have time to harass anyone." Alyssa started to follow Sunny as she made her way back out to the patio.

"You're gonna have to put your big girl panties on eventually and start showing someone your work."

"I know, I know. I'm just not the badgering kind. I don't feel comfortable begging people to give me a chance." If she didn't find a way to change the subject Alyssa was going to badger *her* all night. "Hey, let's put some music on the jukebox."

"I thought you didn't want to sing tonight?" Alyssa looked at her skeptically.

"Playing music doesn't mean I have to sing."

"Well can we at least play our song, cause Renee is here?"

Sunny turned to their friend Renee, "Hey Renee, are you in the mood for a little Joe Cocker?!"

"Hell yeah! Let's do this shit!"

Alyssa ran into the bar to put some songs in. Sunny had a pretty strong feeling that she was going to need to drink a lot of hot tea with honey tomorrow to soothe her throat. Alyssa managed a restaurant/bar called Speakeasy, where different bands would perform. One night after singing at the bar's karaoke night, Sunny's all-time favorite thing to do, Trent a cute guy at the bar, asked her if she would want to sing with him in a little duo that goes to different bars to perform. She thought it sounded awesome, so now they practiced about twice a week and performed one at Speakeasy, sometimes two nights, if they found another bar that would hire them to perform.

Sunny came up with the name Folk You for their little duo. They did covers, he sang and played guitar and Sunny just sang. She had given up on instruments long ago when she realized she wasn't an instant musical genius. They played everything. A little something for everyone, and because of that they had gained a little fan base in the couple of months they'd been playing together. In the process Sunny had developed a serious crush on Trent. And he seemed completely oblivious. *Story of my life.*

Alyssa came running out of the bar. "Our song will be playing next. Get ready bitches!"

Everyone knew what was coming, so they all got a little quieter and moved out of their way. Renee, Alyssa and Sunny moved some of their stuff off the table to make room for banging on it without damaging anything or spilling drinks. They heard the first strains of *A Little Help from my Friends*, the song that was the intro to the show *The Wonder Years*, and their group went completely silent, ready for the hilarity to begin.

First up was Sunny. Each girl got their own part. There was a ton of fists banging and hands slapping on the table and off-key notes. Alyssa screaming at the top of her lungs in imitation of Joe Cocker, was always the best part.

The whole bar busted out laughing and cheering at the girl's antics. Sunny could barely sing anymore, because she was laughing so hard. They finished out the song with a boisterous ending, friends and strangers giving them wild applause. What they lacked in harmony they made up for in enthusiasm.

After the ridiculousness died down the three of them went back into the bar to get another round of drinks.

Renee kept looking back through a section of the glass patio doors in the more secluded part of the patio. "Hey Sunny, I think this super-hot guy keeps eying you up."

"Huh, me?" Sunny looked back towards where Renee's eyes were focused. She literally felt eyes on her and come to think of it Sunny had felt like she was being watched since they had entered the patio, but had shrugged it off as nothing. Thinking it was probably just her friends looking at her.

She could barely make out his face. She could see he had beautiful tanned olive skin with a square jaw that was sporting a nice helping of what she liked to call "man scruff". More than a five-o'clock shadow, but still not a full-on beard, the now popular look that truth be told George Michael started in the early 90's. She could see some jet black wavy hair, but most of his face and hair was covered by the adorable gray wool newsboy hat he wore low on his head. Though most of his face was in shadows he looked vaguely familiar. But it wasn't often she saw anyone that looked quite like that, so she doubted she knew him.

"I can barely see his face. But from what I *can* see, there is *no* freakin' way that he is the slightest bit interested in me! Guys like that don't even know girls like me exist." The blue and white flannel shirt he was wearing did little to hide the massive shoulders and muscle bound arms he had going on. *No freakin' way!*

"I'm telling you, I noticed him when I first got here. And since the moment you guys walked in here his eyes have been on you," Renee persisted.

Sunny looked at Renee like she was smoking crack and said as much. "Renee, you're smokin' crack. And how can you even tell who he's looking at with his hat pulled down so low."

Sunny couldn't help but to sneak another peek. Right when her eyes met the shadowed area where his should be, he lifted his hand to the brim of his hat and nodded at her in acknowledgement. *Holy shit balls Batman!*

"Oh. My. God! Did you just see that?! He totally just acknowledged me!" Her eyes were literally going to bug out of her head.

"I told you!" Renee held her glass up to Sunny's. "Cheers! I think this is about to become a really interesting night."

"Agreed!" Alyssa grinned at Sunny deviously.

They all clinked their glasses together. Sunny tried to smile normally, but it was too late. Panic had set in. Luckily her skin was brown, because she was all kinds of flushed. Palms sweaty, heart pounding, she started up a mantra in her head. *Please don't let him talk to me. Please don't let him talk to me!*

They walked back out to the patio and Sunny sat with her back to him. But she could swear that she could feel his eyes boring into the back of her head. Her hands were so shaky she could barely bring her glass up to her mouth.

Alyssa eyed her curiously. "You should go over and talk to him."

"Ha! You're fucking bat shit crazy, if you think I'm going over there!" Sunny exclaimed nervously.

Alyssa literally spit her vodka cranberry across the table laughing, narrowly missing everyone at the table. She grabbed some napkins to clean up the mess. "Well, with the way he keeps staring at you, it won't be long before he comes over to talk to you."

"I need another beer. Or maybe something stronger. Too bad I hate hard liquor." *Time to make an exception.*

~~~

The situation was bringing back moments of being a majorly insecure teen. There was one moment in particular that stood out in her mind, when Sunny was at a high school basketball game with some friends. They had all left their coats with a friend's mom high up in the bleachers before the game had started, while they chose to sit down below, courtside. Sunny had wanted to go home early, but before she left she needed to get her coat from the upper level bleachers, where the crowd had grown to capacity. She had been frozen with fear at the thought of being called names and fat jokes thrown at her as she walked past. Her mom had come to pick her up and Sunny had run to the car crying and begging her mom to go in and get her coat for her. But her mother being in mixed-matched pajamas, never intending to get out of the car, told Sunny that she had to go in to get her coat.

So once back inside, Sunny had taken a huge breath, put her head down and walked quickly to get her coat. No one had said anything to her, but the fear had made her irrational and nearly paralyzed. That same fear was making a guest appearance tonight, it would seem. Because why else would a guy like that stare at her for any reason, other than to make fun of her.

So a few shots and two more beers later, Sunny was feeling A-Okay. Not drunk, but a slightly happy oblivious barrier had settled over her. He still hadn't made a move from the corner that he was in with a couple of his buddies. But he hadn't stopped staring either. At least, that's what the girls kept telling Sunny. She hadn't built up the courage to even look at him again. And fortunately she had talked the girls out of going to talk to him a hundred times in the last hour and a half.

The girls went in to play more songs. And Sunny heard the first few beats of *I Wanna Dance with Somebody* by Whitney Houston, one of her favorite songs to sing and dance too. The girls came running out and pulled her out of her chair. Wrapped up in the joy of her jam and the slight fog of intoxication, she let loose and danced and sang with all that she had, temporarily forgetting about Tall, Dark and Mysterious over in the corner.

Sunny sang the last notes and swayed her hips as she did a last little turn that put her facing his table directly. Her heart stopped at the beautiful smile that spread across his full lips showing off perfectly straight bright pearly whites. *This fool should be a* Colgate *model, if he isn't already. This* is *California.* With her heart pounding, all she could think was…run! She was in full chicken mode now.

"Uh girls, I'll be right back I have to go to the bathroom." The bar bathroom was just too close to this guy for comfort. So she escaped to the bigger public bathroom around the corner.

Why did the chicken cross the road? To hide from sex on a stick McHottie. That's why! That smile woke up something in Sunny that she had thought died, long ago. Now the gates were slowly opening and she was afraid there just might be a flood. Because though sex might be like riding a bike, and you never forgot, it had been four long years since she'd ridden a "bike" of any kind. And definitely not a "bike" like, *that.*

Sunny had read once that it doesn't matter what you look like, if you believed in your heart that you're a sex goddess, you can please any man in bed. *Ha!* She couldn't quite bring herself to believe she was a sex goddess under normal circumstances, with average guys. But with a guy that looked like *him*…she couldn't even finish the thought. *He's not interested, I'm sure. He probably just thinks I'm cute and entertaining, like most of the guys here in SoCal. Laughing* at *me, not* with *me.*

Finishing her business, Sunny walked out of the stall and washed her hands. Good thing there weren't any mirrors in the bathroom or she was sure she'd freak out over how horrible she looked with this guy around. Looking down as she walked out of the bathroom to make sure she didn't have the ever dreaded toilet paper suck to her shoes, she ran into something. Something…*hard.*

The next few seconds happened as if in slow motion. First Sunny saw a pair of large fairly new blue *Converse.* Then nice and clean relaxed fit jeans on long legs. Further up, a narrow waist encased in *the* blue and white flannel shirt came into her line of sight. Trying to swallow past her suddenly dry throat, her eyes continued their journey upward. Next was a wide chest with crazy cut pectorals that she could make out even through his shirt. She was already craning her neck and hadn't even gotten to his face yet. *How tall is this guy?!* There was a chiseled jaw with the "man scruff", full and sculpted smiling lips, and a straight nose that flooded her senses.

Her first look into his eyes quite literally smacked her down, like a pimp slapping his hoe! They were blue. God were they blue. Not just any blue either. They were like an electric cornflower blue with an outer ring of darker blue around it. And the beauty didn't stop there. He had the most decadently long thick black eyelashes that made the blue that much more striking. Swoon worthy!

Sunny's heart started to pound frantically and radiated heat throughout her entire body. That's when her brain caught up with her eyes and started piecing all his features together. And recognition hit. He brought his index finger up to his full lips. His smooth baritone voice caressed her like the finest silk. "Shh, it's our secret."

Fuck my life! Tall, Dark, and Mysterious was none other than mega-famous movie star Gabriel Wolf!

Chapter 2

Gabe had had a long day of shooting his latest film
Redemption. Nothing had gone quite right all day. He hadn't felt
like he was on his A-game recently. He kept giving shitty take
after shitty take. His co-stars, director, hell the entire film crew
were fed up with his less than stellar performance thus far. He
had no idea what had him in this funk, but he had to get out of it
before they dropped him and brought in someone else to take his
place, contract or not.

So just like any Average Joe, after a rough day of work all he
had wanted to do was to have a couple of beers and relax. A
couple of the guys on the film crew that he'd become friends with
after working on previous movies together, had checked with
some of the locals in Long Beach to see where there was a
reasonably mellow place to have a few drinks. They had been
directed to *Shoreline Village*.

After throwing on a hat and pulling it low over his eyes in
the hopes that no one would recognize him, Gabe and the guys
had set off in that direction. Walking along the harbor; white
boats of varying sizes were bobbing in the water on the right and
restaurants/bars, shops, and even an arcade on the left. But
everything was just a little too busy, 'til they came across a nice
little bar called *Thirty-three Degrees*, with a wraparound patio
that had a relatively secluded section. There were only a handful
of patrons. *Perfect.*

The quiet didn't last long though. One after another, it
looked as though every bartender, server and busboy in the area
stopped in for their own little happy hour. But they kept to

themselves across the patio and didn't give Gabe and his friends a second glance. It seemed as if it was going to be a fairly uneventful night.

Then *she* walked in. Gabe sat up straighter, his eyes zeroed in and the conversation at the table faded out. A mass of wild caramel colored curls framed her face. A plump, voluptuous milk chocolate coated body made his mouth water in anticipation to taste her. And his groin tightened with the need to slide between those beautiful lavish lips or her luscious thighs.

But what made his heart simultaneously stop and drop into his stomach was the most radiant smile he had ever seen. She just simply glowed with a beauty that couldn't be found searching in a mirror, countless hours in the gym or "under the knife". All were common in La-La Land. This woman exuded internal beauty that he had rarely seen since starting his career in Hollywood eighteen years ago. Hell he hadn't even seen it growing up in Michigan. There was very little beauty to be found bouncing from foster home to foster home.

He could tell she was well loved by the reactions of everyone who knew her. Squeals and hugs abound. He thought the crowd was lively before. Apparently her and her friend she came with brought the party. *This should be good.*

"Hey Gabe, have you heard anything we've been talking about?" Dave waved his hand in front of Gabe's face to get his attention.

"Sorry guys." Gabe dipped his head sheepishly.

Tim elbowed Gabe in the side, giving him a sly look. "Where you checking out that hot blonde that just walked in?"

"Actually, no. I was checking out her friend."

"Really? The chubby black girl?!" Tim looked perplexed.

Gabe gave him a warning look that couldn't be mistaken. He already felt protective of her. "Curvaceous, voluptuous and thick would better describe her. Not chubby. She isn't a toddler."

"If you say so", that was from Dave.

"You guys wouldn't know real beauty if she came up to you and tickled your nutsack." Gabe shook his head, turning towards the glass patio doors to look in the bar where the girls were ordering their drinks.

"DAMN!" Tim and Dave shouted at the same time. Though, Gabe had already tuned them out having found more interesting pursuits. The guys just shrugged and continued their earlier conversation about a recent baseball game.

Gabe didn't know what those two were talking about. Couldn't they see what he saw? Hell, it was probably better that they didn't. Less competition.

Gabe watched as the girls came back out to the patio with their drinks. That's when things started to get interesting. The girls cleared the table and all of their friends got quiet. Then the jukebox started playing Joe Cocker's, *A Little Help from My Friends*.

What ensued after that, had to be the cutest and most entertaining thing he'd seen in a long time. It was obvious that these girls had perfected this little performance. Gabe could tell that the other two girls weren't much on singing, but he thought his girl had a beautiful voice. *His girl!* They hadn't even met yet and already he was staking his claim. Well as far as he was concerned, she was already his. It was just a matter of when.

After their song was over, the girls went to grab more drinks. As Gabe watched her, he noticed that one of her friends, a Hispanic looking girl had caught him staring. Her friend started whispering something in her ear and that was when she tried to sneak a peek without making it obvious. Gabe just gave a little smirk, lifted his hand to his hat and tipped his head to her. He chuckled to himself over her reaction. Her eyes widened, mouth dropped open and he could've sworn he saw a flush spread across her cheeks before she quickly whipped her head back around. Modesty. Not something he was accustomed to in his line of work.

Now she started pounding more drinks. Gabe liked to believe that it was because he had affected her, and she was trying to loosen up. He watched her slowly relax. Then as a familiar 80's song started and he watched as her friends pulled her out of her seat to dance. Her body moved and undulated with a smooth grace. Gabe wondered if she would move like that when she was underneath him. The image gave him an instant hard on the likes of which he'd never felt.

As she did her final spin at the end of the song, her body faced his. Gabe couldn't help the predatory grin that spread across his face. Her mouth dropped open, she said a quick word to her friends and then fled out the patio and around the corner. It was time to make his move.

"I'll be back. This may take a minute. So if you guys wanna head back, I'm fine with that", he said to his buddies as an afterthought.

As Gabe walked past the girls' table one shouted, "Go get her cutie" and the other responded with, "Wooohooo!" He just smiled and strode around the corner.

He saw that there was a bathroom, which he assumed was where she had escaped to. *Not for long.* He leaned against the wall that divided the Men's and Women's restrooms on the Women's side. And waited.

He heard water running and a little shuffling. Then she appeared in the doorway, looking down at her feet as she walked. Gabe's heart clenched a little as he realized that she was making sure no toilet paper was stuck to her shoes. *God she's adorable.*

Gabe realized that she wasn't going to look up before she ran into him. So he straightened up at the last second to brace himself. Her incredibly soft large breasts and round face slammed into his stomach and chest. She was so small. Standing at six-foot-four, he had to be over a foot taller than her.

Gabe's hands reached out to help steady her. Feeling her soft curves pressed against him and grasping her soft rounded shoulders to steady her sent every single ounce of blood in his body straight to his cock. Thank the heavens for the jeans he was wearing, because any other material would clearly show the biggest hardest erection he'd ever had.

Slowly she raised her face to his. He was finally able to get a good look at the most stunning honey brown eyes he'd ever seen.

And they saw straight into his soul. His heart started pounding so hard he felt it would beat through his chest.

Gabe was so focused on her eyes that he was able to see the moment she realized who he was. Her eyes flared wide, her breath quickened and her delectable little mouth started opening and closing but no sound escaped. He brought his index finger to his lips, "Shh, it's our secret."

~~~

"Sweet Mary, mother of God! I, uh um ah...," Sunny stammered. *Shit! Think Sunny think.* "Gabriel, uh Mr. Wolf. I um..."

His lips turned up in an adorable smirk...if you can call a smirk adorable. In his case she was sure everything he did was adorable. "You can call me Gabriel. Or just Gabe. No need to be so formal." Sunny just stared at him dumbstruck.

Dammit, I thought I'd be WAY smoother if I did ever meet a celebrity. I guess that theory just flew out the window.

"And your name is?"

Shit, he was still there. And wanted her to speak? "Uh Sunny."

"Sunny?" He looked at her skeptically, like she was pulling a classic girl at a bar move and lying about her name to get rid of an unwelcome guy.

"Um, yes. Madison Stone, actually. My parents didn't think the nickname Maddie suited me. So they called me Sunny, because they said I've always had a sunny disposition. You know Madi-son. Son. Sunny. But instead of an "o" they used a "u"." *Shut up, shut up, SHUT UP! Dammit, first I can't talk at all, now I sound like a rambling idiot!* She internally smacked herself.

He was actually still smiling and not running in the opposite direction. "Sunny. I like it. It suits you perfectly, I think." Her name on his lips felt like silk wrapping around her naked body. She shivered.

"Uh thanks." She knew her vocabulary was way better than

this. *I have got to stop with the ahs, uhs, and ums!* "Sooo is it your movie that they're filming in town? My friend Alyssa mentioned seeing camera crews today." *Sweet, two full sentences with no stumbling!*

"Yeah. A couple of the guys on set wanted to go out and have some drinks after having a rough few days of shooting. We asked around and someone told us about *Shoreline Village*. We liked the way this place looked so we stayed." His voice softened, "I'm glad we did."

Avoiding his last statement she commented on the former. "This is a great place! We come here all the time. It helps that my friend Alyssa is dating the bartender." She couldn't believe he was still here hanging outside of the ladies' room. "Why are you hanging around outside of the ladies' room?" Inner cringe, did she really just ask that?

"Well I saw you run off around the corner and I wanted to make sure your virtue was protected at this late hour. And besides I wanted to get a chance to talk to you without your friends eavesdropping."

"But why? Are you interested in one of them and need my help?"

"No. I think I'm brave enough to talk to a girl on my own."

"Oh. Okay." She looked down unable to look in his eyes any longer. She knew how this worked. Guys like that weren't interested in her. She was accustomed to being the wing-woman in circle of friends. And add to the fact that he was a celebrity and she knew she didn't have a chance. She wasn't even sure she wanted one. *Too scary.*

He brought his hand up to Sunny's chin to gently lift her face back up, her eyes met his. His touch and the words to follow delivered a one-two punch to her gut. "I'm interested in you Sunny. And I didn't want your friends eavesdropping, because I don't need their help to talk to you."

She could've sworn her heart dropped down to her vagina, and started a steady throbbing down there that had her thighs clenching together.

"So ah…you um…" *God bless America!* At that point she just squeezed her eyes shut to block out his face so she could think. Fat bit of good that did her! His face was now burned into her retinas.

"You're adorable." She heard the smile in his voice.

"Yeah well you're stupid fucking sexy." Her eyes popped open as she clapped both hands over her mouth. *You. Have. Got. To. Be. Kidding! Did I really just utter those words?* She must have because his head was thrown back and his shoulders were shaking with laughter.

He wiped the tears from his eyes and his laughter settled into a soft chuckle. "You're a breath of fresh air Sunny!"

"I would think you'd be running away screaming at this point. I either can't talk at all, or babbling, or saying completely inappropriate things. You should walk away now, before I embarrass myself any further." She tried looking everywhere but at him.

He stepped closer to her. "Run? No I don't think so. And I like the inappropriate things you say. In fact I can't wait to hear the next crazy thing that comes out of that delectable mouth." Again he grabbed her chin and forced her face up to his and her insides liquefied when she looked into those ridiculous blue eyes and saw...lust. *Lust? At me?!* "You have the most amazing lips I think I've ever seen."

Finally, a man that appreciated her lips. His face started to inch towards hers, but at the last minute she turned and gave him her cheek. *Damn! Now why did I go and do that? Why, I know why. Because once his lips touch mine I'm a goner and would probably be in and then out of his bed in two seconds flat. And I'd just be another notch on his bedpost. And I'm pretty sure that is one gnarled bedpost. So no matter how famous and drop-dead gorgeous he is I deserve better than that. Must. Stay. Strong.*

Just a little pissed off that he would try to take such liberties with her so soon after meeting her, Sunny actually forgot all about her star-struck state of mind to let him have it. Putting her hands on his sizable chest and giving a little push. *Jesus, Mary and Joseph I've never felt pecs like that in my life! Focus.*

"Look here buddy. I don't care who you are, you just don't go around taking kisses like they're free or something! I deserve better than that. I'm not a prude or super old school or anything like that, but I deserve a date first. And no, I'm not a gold-digger either. But a man shows that he respects and appreciates a woman by taking her out on a date, first. Not by mauling her before he's even bought her a drink, at the very least!" Oh Lord, had she just really berated Gabriel Wolf, superstar extraordinaire? Like he'd really take her out on a date? Great! She hadn't had sex in four years and not only did she just push a guy completely away. And this particular guy, any woman would jump at the chance to be in his bed at least once. Well it was too late to take it back now.

"Okay," he said softly. Sunny's eyes shot up to his and her jaw fell to the floor when she saw the sheepish but somewhat impressed look on his face. He probably was used to getting whatever he wanted.

"Okay?"

"Yes. I was a jerk. What time should I pick you up tomorrow?" His face was completely and unbelievably sincere.

"Well I have to work all day. And then after that I have a show at Speakeasy. And don't you have a movie to shoot?" *Am I really having this conversation right now?!* He. Gabriel Wolf. Was asking *her* out on a date?! Never, even in her most vivid imaginations would she have guessed this would happen when she woke up this morning. Wasn't she just drowning herself in *Ben & Jerry's* about three hours ago?

"Yes. But tomorrow we're only filming during the day. You have a show? Doing what?" He seemed genuinely interested. *Boggles the mind.*

"I'm in a little music duo called Folk You. Don't laugh! We do covers and play just about anything." Sunny smiled slightly at the broad grin that spread across his face.

"Folk You?" He struggled not to laugh. "That's an awesome name! I love your voice. What time do you start?"

"Nine. And we play 'til eleven. But you're not going to come are you? I don't think I'd be able to concentrate knowing you're in the audience." Sunny said in a panic at the thought.

She could've sworn a slightly hurt expression crossed his face. But it was gone before she could be sure. "Then what about the next night, Friday? I'm actually off the entire day. I'm not in the scenes they'll be shooting that day."

"I don't work at all on Friday either."

"That settles it then. You're spending the day with me."

"I uh, well um…shit! How do you know I don't have plans that day? I might have to do laundry or wash my hair or something."

His eyes twinkled with the knowledge that he had her. "Do you? Have plans, that is?"

"Well no, but-"

He interrupted her, "But nothing. I'm taking you out to have a good time and show you that I can be a complete gentleman." A few seconds ticked by as he held her gaze with those eyes. She couldn't take it.

"Okay, fine."

"Good. Now shall we get back before your friends think you've been kidnapped?" She started nodding her head, completely disoriented from the last five minutes. That's when he whipped off his hat, bowed at the waist while grabbing her hand and kissing it. *Lord, help me. I am totally and utterly fucked!* Just the act of him finally revealing all his hair had her mesmerized. It was a luxurious head of jet black, thick, and wavy hair. It could easily rival Patrick *"McDreamy"* Dempsey's hair. The last movie she saw him in, it was cut short for the role he played and it was hot like that too. But now her fingers itched to touch it, to run her fingers through it. She could just imagine pulling it while his head was between her…*STOP! Stay strong.* Spending any time alone with this man was going to be hazardous to her health. She just knew it.

As they walked back to the bar he was close enough to her that their arms kept brushing back and forth. And even though there were clothes between their skin it did little to help the flip flops going on in her stomach.

Sunny peeked up at him nervously. "So...should I not mention who you are to my friends? They'll be dying to know details."

They rounded the corner to the patio, which had cleared out quite a bit. "Well, seeing as how the crowd has dwindled down. I don't think it'll be a problem. I just wanted a quiet evening without being bombarded by a lot of questions, autographs and selfies."

There were a few people inside the bar. But just Alyssa, Renee and Renee's boyfriend Marco were left on the patio. As they walked up, the girls were grinning all over themselves and ready to burst with questions.

"Uh, hey guys." Sunny fidgeted nervously, this was going to be interesting. "So this is Gabriel...Wolf."

Gabriel pushed his hat back on his head bringing his whole face into the light. Sunny scrunched up her face in anticipation as she heard their sharply drawn in gasps.

"Holy shit!"

"What the...?!"

"No way!"

They all spoke at once, so she couldn't tell who said what.

"Gabriel, this is Alyssa, Renee and Marco." Sunny pointed to each one as she said their names. And in kind Gabriel reached out to shake their hands.

"Nice to meet you guys." He was totally at ease with their astonishment and just brushed it off as nothing.

"Uh huh."

"Y-yeah."

"Mm hmm."

Sunny was pretty sure that she heard them sigh, even Marco! Well at least she wasn't the only one that lost all motor function when around him.

As Sunny and Gabe took two seats next to each other at the table she noticed the table where Gabriel and his buddies had been, was empty. "Hey, where did your friends go?"

"Oh they were getting pretty tired. So before I went to find where you had run off too, I just told them to head back home. I'll get a cab later." A beautiful smile spread across his face.

"You should've been a *Colgate* toothpaste model." *She* should probably stop saying everything that crossed her mind.

"Look who's talking! You have a breathtaking smile, Sunny. It was the first thing I noticed about you when you walked onto this patio." The compliment sent shivers down her spine. Dammit, but she didn't know if she liked this feeling. *I'm an optimistic person, but this is just too much.*

"Uh thanks." She'd never been completely comfortable with compliments. And was really uncomfortable now, coming from an incredibly gorgeous man that sees million dollar smiles on a daily basis. Literally, because she was sure the dentists in Hollywood got paid millions to keep those pearly whites bright.

"So what do you do Sunny? Besides singing gigs at night and charming the pants off of every guy you encounter?" Sunny gapped at him as if he were crazy. Gabriel's eyes were focused completely on her. His long-lashed blue eyes seemed to pierce into her soul. It was seriously unnerving.

Sunny shrugged, always embarrassed by the answer to this question. "I work in retail. Nothing special. And trust me I don't 'charm the pants off of' anyone."

Gabriel leaned forward capturing Sunny's gaze and holding it, letting her know he meant business. "I doubt that. Maybe they're just too stupid to admit or realize it. The guys here in SoCal can be pretty dense and insecure, looking for supermodels to validate their self-worth."

She looked away, unable to hold the connection.

Realizing Sunny's discomfort he changed the subject. "So why do you work in retail? With your personality and talent you should be doing something else. And by what I can tell from the short amount of time I've known you, you seem pretty intelligent."

"She's actually a writer!" Alyssa piped in. "She wants to write… Ouch!" Sunny kicked Alyssa under the table, cutting her short. Gabe looked curiously at Alyssa.

"You write? What do you-"

Sunny cut him off, "I don't know how you can tell I'm intelligent. I have barely been able to form two proper sentences since you first spoke to me." Unfortunately he didn't realize that this subject made her just as uncomfortable as the previous one. And Sunny didn't want him to know that she wrote screenplays. She didn't want him to think that she was interested in him for what he could do for her career.

He smiled at that. "Trust me I can tell. Plus, stupid people don't have a whole lot going on behind the eyes. Like it's all blank in there, or something. There's a whole lot of thought going on behind your eyes. It has me dying to figure out just what you're thinking. Though, I think I already know."

"I hope not." Sunny looked down at her pint glass, trying to be more interested in the condensation sliding down the sides. She felt like she was all of a sudden under a microscope.

Gabe reached his hand out and his thumb caressed a path down the side of Sunny's cheek. When he reached her chin, he tipped her face up to his forcing her to look at him once again. "Sunny, you're like an open book. And I already know the story. But I want to read it anyway."

Well....shit! That had to be the most amazing line she'd ever heard. Hands down! He couldn't be serious. He looked serious. He was also an amazing actor. But why take the time out to bamboozle *her*. She was no one. This was all so confusing.

Sunny's friends were no help. They were completely silent. Their heads were moving back and forth, like they were watching a tennis match. Their mouths hanging open in wonder. She hoped they all had a bug fly in their mouths.

Feeling uncomfortable with the whole situation she stood up. "I think I need another beer. I'll be right back."

She quickly made her way towards the bar. A large hand on her arm stopped her as she stepped through the doorway. She looked up to see Gabe's face filled with worry as he pulled her towards a quiet corner. "Hey, are you alright? Did I say something to upset you?"

Closing her eyes and taking a deep breath Sunny went for it. "Look, I don't think it's a good idea for us to go on that date Friday."

"And why not?"

"Because I don't like being made a fool of, that's why!" Gesturing from his head to his toes and back again. "And because you're...you." Then sweeping her hands from her head to toes in disgust, "And I'm this! Guys that look like you don't look at girls like me. And those are guys that aren't even famous, with ladies lined up around the corner waiting for even a passing glance to tell their friends about. I don't know why you've taken an interest in me. Isn't there some smokin' hot actress or supermodel you should be dating? Because this", she waved her hand between the two of them, "is bound to end in disaster."

"You don't see yourself very clearly, do you?"

"No, that's where you're wrong Gabriel. I see myself very clearly. A face that can pass for pretty and a chubby body with a fan-freakin-tastic personality. But it's when I look at myself through a man's eyes, that it all becomes glaringly clear. 'Fun to flirt with and make a couple of harmless passes at, but when it comes down to who I want on my arm in public, only a walking talking *Barbie* doll will do.'"

His jaw was clenched and ticked as if in anger. "You're comparing me to a bunch of blind insecure assholes! I have a mind to kiss you senseless just to show you how desirable you are." She opened her mouth to protest, but he stopped her. "But I promised to take you on a proper date first. In the few hours since I first laid eyes on you, you've blown every woman I've ever met out of the water. Your parents were right to name you Sunny, because something about you radiates light. Everyone around you sees it, even the guys, but they're either: too intimidated or awestruck to admit it. But not me."

He raised his hand to her face and she held her breath. He stroked his thumb down her cheek to her chin. She must have looked like a deer in headlights. "I just don't get it."

"Sunny, I've been surrounded by the most; shallow, insipid, devious and manipulative 'beautiful' females you could imagine. And I've never been ashamed to say it 'til now, but I've had them all in my bed. I need this. To be around you." Gabe said, staring deeply into her soul.

Sunny was still skeptical. How do you go from being ignored by the general male population, to being pursued by *People* magazine's *Sexiest Man Alive* and not think that you're being *Punk'd*? *Oh what the hell!* More than likely she'd end up brokenhearted. But at least she'd be brokenhearted with a great story.

"So you're sure I'm not being *Punk'd*?"

For the second time that night, Gabe threw back his head in laughter. Then he grabbed her face in both hands…huge hands, which basically covered the majority of her face. And he gently kissed the tip of her nose. "You're amazing. Now let's get you one more beer and then I'll take you home." He took her hand in his and pulled her over to the bar.

Chapter 3

Gabe couldn't believe the turn the whole day had taken. All for the better. He even felt more inspired, and couldn't wait to get back on the movie set to see if his performance would improve. All of this was because of the woman walking next to him.

Sunny had let him buy her another beer. He loved how unpretentious and down-to-earth she was. *A girl in Southern California that willingly drank cheap beer? Even when someone else was paying? Huh?* Gabe knew he was being somewhat unfair to the California girls, *somewhat*. But considering the females he was surrounded by, if someone was buying, the guy in question better believe that it was going to be top shelf booze or high-end wine.

As the bar had closed, her friend Alyssa decided to stay while her boyfriend closed down, so that Gabe could walk Sunny home alone. He was grateful to her friend.

She didn't say much on the way, except for a few words to guide him in the right direction of her building. Gabe could tell that she was deep in thought. He just hoped that they were good thoughts and not thinking up other excuses to get out of going on a date with him.

He couldn't believe how someone as beautiful as Sunny would think so badly about herself. Gabe felt a very real rage radiate through him. He wanted to punch every guy that made her feel less than amazing, in the throat. He unclenched his fists, and tried to calm his mind. He started to realize that maybe the crappy way she was treated in the past would only be to his advantage. Because when he was through, she'd have no doubt that he very much meant everything he said and did and that she was beautiful.

"Why are you so quiet?" Gabe looked down at her. "I hope you're not trying to find another reason not to go out with me."

Sunny stopped in front of an old, cool looking building that Gabe knew had to have been built in the 1920's. She turned to look up at him, "This is me." She bit down on her bottom lip, making Gabe do an internal groan. Unaware what she was doing to him she continued, "No, I'm not thinking of another reason. I was just trying to process this whole crazy night." She shook her head, as if trying to clear it. "But anyway, thanks for the beer and walking me home. You didn't have to do that."

"Yes I did. I wanted to." Gabe reached up to brush Sunny's curls away from her face. Her eyes fluttered shut. Then he brought his hands up and gently placed his fingers on the back of her neck. Thumbs caressing her cheeks, he turned her face slightly and bent down to kiss her left cheek. Then he turned her face in the other direction and kissed the other cheek. With each touch of his lips to her skin he could hear her sudden indrawn breaths. He was so turned on he could hardly see straight. But out of respect for her wishes, he pulled himself together. Stepped back and released her neck with a gentle slide of his fingers against her soft skin. And her body quivered in response. *Patience.*

~~~

Of all the times for her to have decided to show some restraint and not fall into bed with a man (her two mistakes in her previous relationships), this seemed like a really shitty time according to her soaking wet panties. It took every ounce of strength that she had not to jump his bones. Aside from the fact that he was a mega-star that she'd drooled over for several years, he was drop dead gorgeous *and* sweet. And being up close and personal with him turned her fairy-tale crush, into a very real one. *Also, I haven't had sex in four fucking years....that has got to be some kind of record!*

Gabriel Wolf was her idea of perfection. She had become so tired of the metro-sexual girlie-men that seemed to be the norm these days. Gabe was *all* man. He had to have been about six-foot-four, two-hundred and forty pounds of solid muscle, with a casual style and grace that was very much low maintenance. Lumberjack/Linebacker meets *Christian Grey* or maybe Superman, her all-time favorite superhero. *Yum.*

Gabe slid his hands from her neck, sending shudders through Sunny's whole body. *He's got great hands. I wonder how they would feel caressing my...no, no, NO! That is a slippery slope into Slutsville, closely followed by No Call Town.*

Stepping back, Sunny put some distance between them. "So what time is good for you Friday?"

"How about I pick you up around one in the afternoon?"

"One? Why so early?" Sunny wondered if maybe he wanted to get the date out of the way so that he could ditch her early to enjoy the rest of his night, warming his bed with some hot model.

Gabe seemed to study her for a second. "Sunny, we both have the day off Friday, and I want to spend as much time with you as I can. To be honest I wanted to say nine in the morning. Hell six a.m. would be perfect! But I thought maybe you'd actually like to get some sleep, knowing you'll have a late night tomorrow. Stop doubting the fact that I want to be around you."

Sunny couldn't believe how well he was already reading her. She guessed she was an 'open book'. "Sorry. This is just weird for me. Sooo, is there any particular dress code I should know about?"

"Just dress comfortably."

Sunny rolled her eyes at him. "I am a girl, you know. You have to be more specific than that. A dress and flat sandals, for a walk on the beach, comfortable? Or jeans and gym shoes, to go hiking, comfortable?"

The smile that spread across Gabe's face almost stopped her heart. "I guess dress and sandals, comfortable." He paused and his eyes narrowed. "Wait a minute. You said gym shoes. I haven't heard that since I left Michigan. Where are you from Sunny?"

"Illinois."

"I knew you weren't from California! Level-headed, down-to-earth, drinks cheap beer even when someone else is buying. A Midwest girl." He took a step closer to her.

She backed away a step. "The best kind of girl." She winked at him.

Sunny was no match for his speed. He took a quick step towards her, grabbed her by the waist with his left hand and brought his right hand up to caress her face. Which she was realizing, was his favorite thing to do. She felt a telltale hardness against her thigh. But her arousal was no match for the insecurity she felt with his hand around her thick waist.

Squirming out of his grasp, "I better get inside. I have a long day tomorrow. I need some sleep." She backed away towards the door of her apartment building. A wistful smile on her lips.

"Oh wait!" Gabe strode towards her. "Lemme see your phone." This was not a request. His hand was outstretched, expecting her to obey his command. She kind of liked it. A man that knew what he wanted and went for it. She smiled to herself and handed over her phone.

He took her phone, programmed his number into her phone, called himself with it and then programmed her name into his phone. *Holy shit! I have Gabriel Wolf's number! Unreal.*

"Perfect. Now you can't escape me." He grinned slyly. "Alright, I'll let you get some sleep. Goodnight, Sweet Girl." He leaned down and kissed Sunny's forehead, lingering slightly. As if he just couldn't let her go. *Aw, HELL!*

Sunny knew there was no way in hell that she was getting any sleep tonight. She hoped that the rasp in her throat from lack of sleep, made her voice sound sexy tomorrow, instead of like she swallowed a frog.

"Goodnight, Gabriel." She turned and walked into her building. She could feel his eyes watching her through the windows of the lobby. *Just don't trip.*

Chapter 4

"Cut!" The director yelled. Kyle Higgins was a new up and coming director. He was in his mid-thirties; medium height, skinny, with horn-rimmed glasses. Gabe liked him. He worked well with the cast and crew alike. Giving more praise, than barking orders and criticism. Kyle made his way over to Gabe. "That was really great Gabe. I don't know what you did to get your mind back in the game, but keep it up."

Sunny. It seemed weird to Gabe that one tiny little spitfire of a woman could inspire him so much. *But hey, I might as well go with it.*

The last thing he thought of before he fell asleep last night and the first thing on his mind when he woke up this morning was Sunny. And since she was on his mind and because he knew how unsure she was of his intentions, he made sure that he had sent her a "Good Morning" text.

Gabe: *Good morning, Sweet Girl.*

Sunny: *Good morning, Gabriel. How r u?*

Gabe: *I'm doing well. I'll be better when I see you tomorrow.*
;)

Little did she know that Gabe, had plans to sneak in to see her perform tonight. He had wrapped up the text conversation with her to let her get ready for work, with the anticipation of seeing her later.

~~~

It had been a normal day in retail hell for Sunny. Getting

yelled at by uppity customers that thought they were entitled to any and everything. But she couldn't remember the last time she had smiled *this* much. Remembering the previous night and the following texts that morning, had her grinning from ear to ear.

Her co-workers seemed to notice, and asked frequently why she was glowing. But Sunny wasn't ready to reveal her rapidly increasing and exciting new love life. No sense in counting her chickens before they hatched. Her situation with Gabriel Wolf was too new and quite frankly dreamlike to know exactly where it was all heading.

And she knew that there would be haters, so why give them something to revel in when things didn't work out. Which, she couldn't see how it would work out.

All she could do now was stop worrying about it, and just except it for what it was. Something new and mind-blowing. She tamped down the growing butterflies in her stomach, waved goodbye to her work friends to head home to get ready for her gig later tonight.

~~~

Walking into the bar, Sunny saw Trent setting up for the show. Walking over to the stage, she realized that seeing him for the first time since meeting and spending time with Gabe, Trent was just plain old mediocre in comparison. It was a nice feeling after being ignored by him romantically for six months.

Trent was average height, leaning more towards the short side of average. He was skinny with light brown hair, hazel eyes and a nice smile. But now, she was blinded by the image of piercing blue eyes, made that much more striking framed by jet black eyelashes, winged brows and wavy *McDreamy* hair.

"Hey, Trent."

"Oh hey, Sunny. You look nice tonight."

"Thanks." A day ago she would've swooned over the compliment, looking deeper into it for more than what it was.

For the show tonight she had chosen one of her favorite

dresses. It was a black with white polka dot flowy number that stopped right below her knees, with a keyhole back. The neckline was plunging, so it showed off a great deal of her cleavage. And she paired it with faux suede wedge heels, with a wide belt, large hoop earrings and a pretty silk flower that held back one side of her wild curls.

All the accessories were in a fun hot pink. Obviously hot pink was one of her favorite colors to wear. The hot pink wedges were pushed upon her by Alyssa and though she hated heels and they killed her feet, she had to admit that this dress was made for these heels. Not to mention the fact that they made her short and pudgy legs look long and supple. Sacrificing her comfort for this one dress just might be worth the pain. She felt great, even beautiful. And she kind of wished that she hadn't discouraged Gabe from coming tonight.

Sunny and Trent spent the next half hour doing a sound check and downing a few drinks to calm the preshow jitters they always got, no matter how many shows they did. During that time Sunny could tell that Trent was puzzled over her lack of attention to him. No more coy eyes or shy smiles. *Get used to it jackoff...you've been replaced.*

"Are you alright, Sunny?" Trent asked hesitantly.

"Oh I'm great actually. Why do you ask?" Sunny asked innocently.

"Uh, no reason. You just seem...preoccupied."

Ha! 'Preoccupied'! I'm in down-right oblivion. "No, I'm good. Just daydreaming I guess. So...you ready to get this party started?"

"Yeah. Let's give 'em what they want." He winked at Sunny, and then turned around to make his way to the stage.

Sunny slammed the last of her beer, set the empty pint glass on the bar and followed Trent to the stage. Some Folk You fans were already gathered in front. Sunny now on stage behind the mike, she looked out into the steadily growing crowd and smiled. *I love this.*

"Hey, everybody! Are you ready to have a great night?!"

Sunny shouted into the mike.

"Woo…" The little crowd in the front shouted back.

"Oh, come on! That was pathetic! I said, are you ready to have a great fucking night?!"

This time the entire bar went up in a raucous chorus.

"Now that's what I'm talkin' about! We're Folk You, and we are pleased to give you exactly what you want."

Trent strummed out the first few chords of *Blister in the Sun*. The crowd went nuts hearing the beloved classic. As Sunny started to sing, people were scrambling to move tables to the side. When the area was clear…the dancing commenced.

~~~

Gabe walked into the crowded darkened bar, decorated in blood red walls and black furnishings. Rock 'n roll paraphernalia adorned the walls; from guitars, to drumsticks and posters. The place screamed 'music venue'. And dead center on stage above a decent sized group of couples slow dancing was Sunny crooning *Let's Get It On*.

When he saw her for the first time the previous night, she had been dressed casually. The look coming across as sweet and trying somewhat to conceal her sensuality.

Now Gabe nearly swallowed his tongue at the sight of her. She was in some floaty knee-length polka dot dress, with a plunging neckline. The swells of her breasts looked so creamy and chocolaty and inviting. Her smooth calves were muscled, shapely and glistening as if she had put some oil on them to make them shine. And they looked so much longer than he remembered, which was probably due to the hot pink, 'come fuck me' heels she had on. *Oh, to have those gleaming calves resting on my shoulders with my face buried between her silken thighs, with those heels still on.* His jeans grew rather snug and he almost came on the spot from that image. *Yes please!*

Her hair was what seemed to be her normal sexy mane of wild curls surrounding her face and shoulders. Made more, soft and alluring with the pink flower holding back one side. Her eyes were closed and passion was etched deep into her face, feeling every word she sang. And Gabe imagined that her face would look every much like that when he was buried deep inside of her. He knew he was going to have to stop thinking like that, or he wouldn't be able to walk in a minute.

Foregoing any drinks because he knew he had to drive home in a couple hours and not wanting to risk anyone recognizing him up at the bar. Gabe pulled his baseball cap further down to hide his face as he made his way over to a private table in a dark corner that had a good view of the stage and *Sunny*.

~~~

Sunny felt chills race down her spine and goosebumps spread across her skin, though she was on fire from singing under the hot stage lights. There was only one time that she had felt her body react that way. Last night. *Gabriel.* When, he had stared at her from across the patio. The feeling had unnerved her. He made her feel unlike any man had previously. And that's when she knew. *He has to be here!* She wouldn't feel this way otherwise.

As she sang she casually looked around the bar. It was hard to see with the bright lights in her eyes. But as the rotating colorful lights shifted, she was able to make out a dark figure sitting in the corner watching her. It had to be him. Her voice gave the slightest quiver as she sang the last notes.

When the song was over, she looked over at Trent, silently communicating that it was time for a quick break. Slipping his guitar strap from around his neck, Trent addressed the crowd. "Alright folks, we're gonna take a short break. Be back in fifteen."

With trembling fingers, Sunny replaced the mike back on its stand and exited the stage. She made her way over to the bar to grab her drink that the bartender had waiting for her. And with a shaky exhale of breath, she made her way over to the dark corner.

Sunny stopped in front of his seated form. He was wearing a

black baseball cap pulled low, once again covering half of his face, emphasizing his 'man scruff' coated square jaw and his full rather pink lips. A fairly fitted gray Henley that showed off every single bulging muscle in his shoulders, arms and torso, with distressed and faded jeans covering what she was pretty sure were massive muscular legs and immaculate white gym shoes. He looked absolutely delicious, and completely unpretentious, considering his stardom.

"Gabriel," she said sounding all breathy, even to her own ears.

His bowed capped head made a slow rise up her body and she realized that he was literally devouring her with his eyes. When his stunning blue gaze finally made its way to her face, what she saw there took her breath away. Hunger. Pure, simple, and unadulterated *hunger*.

His long body unfolded from the chair, until he towered over her. Overwhelmed her. Even in her heels. Barely an inch stood between them.

"You look good enough to eat. All chocolate confection with hot pink toppings." He placed his hand lightly on the slope of her stomach over her dress, his fingers pointing downward. His hand slid down further until his fingertips gently touched the top of her clenching sex.

"I wonder what other parts of you are hot and pink", he whispered into her ear.

Sunny gasped and knees buckled. Gabe's reflexes were quick, and he encircled her in his strong arms to catch her before she face-planted on the floor. To an outsider, it looked as if he was just giving her a hug. They both knew better.

"I've got you." Gabe spoke softly against her hair. "It's good to know that I affect you as much as you-"

"Hey Sunny. Who's this", an accusing voice interrupted behind Sunny.

Trent. *Are you fucking kidding me!* Gabe's arms relaxed around Sunny's waist enough for her to turn, but not enough to let go. The possessiveness of the move made her smile on the inside.

"Hey Trent. This is…uh…" Shit! Now what? She didn't want to actually tell him who Gabe was and blow his guise. He obviously didn't want anyone to know who he was. She respected his privacy.

Gabe relinquished one arm to extend his hand to shake Trent's. "Gabe. Gabriel Wolf. And you are?" Sunny could read between the lines. And his tone said, *'That's right…the movie star. And who the fuck are you?'*

"You mean *the* Gabriel Wolf, as in the movie star?!" Trent was dumbstruck. *Or just plain dumb.* Sunny thought, still pissed over the interruption.

"Yep. One and the same."

"Well, I'm Trent. I play with Sunny in the band. She never told me that she knew you." Trent glanced at her with a hurt expression on his face.

Hurt. I gave him every opportunity to ask me out, and the first time I get hit on by a megastar or anyone for that matter, he's all of a sudden hurt because I've moved on?! Gimme a break!

"I actually just met him last night, Trent." Sunny said in mild exasperation.

"Well, you looked pretty cozy after *just* meeting him." Trent said in a snotty insinuating tone.

Gabe stepped around Sunny, putting her behind him. Obviously about to squash the situation before it got ugly. "*Well,* seeing as how it's none of your business what she does…unless you're *with* her?" Gabe turned to look down at Sunny questioningly. Worry briefly crossing his handsome face. She shook her head 'no' quickly. He turned back around, relief relaxing his posture. "She says 'no'. And since there's nothing between you two, I would strongly suggest you stick to playing your guitar."

Damn! He meant business. She liked it…someone finally wanting her. And he wasn't afraid to admit it or stand up for her. *Who da thunk?*

~ 40 ~

"She did have feelings for me before she met you, ya know?" *Dude, really? Give up already! He's the most gorgeous man on the planet...do you really think you have a chance at this point?!*

"Well then I'd say you missed your shot. Because I've got her now, and I don't plan on being dumb enough to let her go." *Cocky much?* Eh, who was she kidding, he did have her. Hook line and sinker.

Trent glared at them, and then stormed off in a huff.

"That was pleasant." Sunny said sarcastically. Then she made a show of smelling herself.

"What are you doing?" Gabe looked down at her like she'd lost her mind.

"Just checking to make sure I don't smell like pee. Because that was definitely a pissing match." She gave him a cheeky little smile.

He burst into a deep rumbling laugh. "Sorry. He kinda pissed me off." Pause. "You really *liked* that dick?!"

"Guilty. Though I don't know why. He just acted like such a brat! He's never given me the time of day. And now that I'm getting attention from someone else, now he wants to get all possessive. Fuck that noise!" Sunny cringed. "Sorry. I have a bit of a potty-mouth sometimes."

"Don't apologize. It's cute. You're a little spit-fire when you want to be." He wrapped her up in his arms again. She enjoyed his hard warmth.

"I think my fifteen minutes was up a while ago. Better get back." Sunny said shyly.

"Alright. I guess I can share you with the masses. But I don't have to like it." He sighed and released her reluctantly.

Talk about sharing with the masses. If this thing, this attraction went anywhere, Sunny knew she had to share him with the *world*. Which she wasn't really sure she could do.

~~~

Gabe watched as Sunny made her way back to the stage. He nearly went over to the stage himself to punch Trent in the face after the scowl he gave Sunny. *Little prick!* Gabe didn't particularly like her being around Trent, but he would never purposely try to ruin something that obviously meant a lot to her. She loved performing.

Before they started the next song, Trent effectively put the kibosh on the rest of the evening.

"Ladies and gentlemen. Before we start our last set, I just wanted to let everyone know that we have a special guest in the house. The very talented actor…Gabriel Wolf!" A calculating smile spread across Trent's face as he pointed in Gabe's direction.

The crowd went nuts and Gabe was bum-rushed by adoring if not slightly overzealous fans, leaving the once packed dance floor empty in front of Sunny. The manager and bouncers tried to make their way through the crowd to help him. But it was near impossible.

Finally muscling their way in, they grabbed Gabe, surrounding him while trying to make their way to the exit. The manager must have called the cops, because he saw flashing red and blue lights enter the parking lot. Before being pushed through the doorway, Gabe looked back at the stage. Sunny was in Trent's face having a heated discussion, anger radiated off of her. And then she turned and threw the mike down on the floor and stormed off. Even in the chaos he could hear the loud thump of the mike hitting the floor reverberating through the speakers. The sound ending the night with disappointing finality.

~~~

"What the hell was that Trent?!" Sunny glared.

"That dude is just using you, Sunny. I'm just doing you a favor before he hurts you. You can't really believe that someone like him would date you? He dates supermodels and hot actresses." Trent looked down his noses at Sunny self-righteously.

Sunny stepped back as if she'd been slapped, his words hitting to close to her doubts about Gabe's interest in her. "You're a fucking asshole, Trent!" Sunny yelled into Trent's face. "You knew I had feelings for you and you didn't give me the time of day. Now that I have someone interested in me that's ten times better than you'll ever be in every way, NOW you want to act like you care?! You can go to hell. Find someone else to sing with. I'm done!" Sunny threw the mike down and stormed off the stage, leaving Trent gaping in shock.

Tears threatened to pour down her face as she made her way through the back exit. She managed to hold them back until she got to her car. "Asshole, asshole, ASSHOLE!" She slammed her hand against the steering wheel, punctuating the word each time she sobbed it.

Pushing aside her dejected mood, Sunny needed to know if Gabe was okay. Reaching back, she grabbed her purse that was hidden on the floor behind the passenger seat. She searched through her purse for her phone. Finally finding it at the bottom, she wiped her face with the backs of her hands so that she could see the screen as she called up his number.

"Hello, Sweet Girl." Gabe said picking up after the first ring.

"I'm so sorry Gabe. Are you okay?" Sunny said trying to control the teary tremble in her voice, but failing miserably.

"I'm fine, Sunny. Don't worry about me and don't apologize for that fucker. If I had the chance I would've karate chopped him in the throat for you!" He growled indignantly, like a little kid.

Sunny burst into a fit of giggles, tears forgotten. He was trying to cheer her up. And it worked. "Thanks I needed that laugh."

"No problem. I love your laugh. And anything I can do to hear it again, I'll gladly do it. But I was dead serious. I see that dude again and he's losing an Adam's apple."

Sunny's head fell back on the headrest, the laughter shaking her whole body. Now tears of a different kind streamed down her face.

"Stop! Stop! It hurts!" Sunny grabbed her aching stomach.

"What? You didn't know I'm a ninja by night…roundhouse kicking fools and ripping out their throats?"

"Ha! You didn't describe a ninja. You just described Patrick Swayze in *Roadhouse*! Which is a favorite of mine. I own it."

"Hmm. Do I sense a movie-buff in my midst?"

"Yes, Mr. Movie Star, you do. Care to play me in a friendly game of *Scene It* sometime? I have a current record of 7-in-0, by the way", Sunny challenged smugly.

"Oh ho! Bring it baby! Name the place, name the date and time. And I'll be there, spankin' that ass!" She shivered at the thought. She was no *Anastasia Steele*, but being bent over his lap at his mercy did have some appeal.

"I'll let you know. Just be prepared. Maybe do a little studying, you'll need it." She loved the playful banter they were having back and forth. It almost felt like they'd known each other for years.

"How about you get home and get prepared for tomorrow, because I plan on wearing you out." Her stomach dropped and apparently released bats as opposed to butterflies, as violent as her stomach was fluttering. *Did that mean he plans on trying to have sex with me? Am I ready for that? Am I ready for him to see me naked? Is it too soon? Dear God, I can't have another sleepless night!*

Her silence stretched out a little too long. Gabe hesitantly responded to her silence. "Sunny? I didn't mean that the way it sounded. I just meant I have a long day planned for you. There's no pressure to move it to the next level."

"Promise?" Sunny asked shakily.

"Aw, baby. I promise." Sunny could hear the desperation in his voice for her to believe him.

"Okay. I'll see you tomorrow at one?"

"Yeah. One o'clock. Goodnight, Sweet Girl."

"Goodnight, Gabriel."

Sunny pressed the end button on her phone and headed home for another restless night.

Chapter 5

Traffic was light this time of day as Gabe coasted down the freeway, on his way to pick up Sunny for their much anticipated first date. Deciding what to do on their date had been a slight bump in the road. He knew that she would be impressed by something super fancy, but at the same time overwhelming for someone as down-to-earth and practical as Sunny. He needed to find something to do that matched her personality. Fun, exciting, and understated sexy. He was pretty sure his final decision would make the perfect first date.

For the first half of the date, he had decided to wear a pair of nice dark-washed jeans, a plain white fitted t-shirt and his white *Nikes*. And of course, for a little anonymity, a black baseball cap. For the night portion of the date, he brought a long sleeve blue button-down dress shirt and a pair of black dress shoes to go with the jeans he was already wearing. He was sure that anything Sunny wore would work for both day and night.

Pulling up in front of her building, he realized that he was nervous. Really nervous. Like a 'high school kid on his first date'-nervous. He knew that this date was make it or break it. Sunny was like trying to coax a wild animal to eat out of your hand. One wrong move and she'd run. No woman had ever acted like this around him. Most times he had to beat them off with a stick. Not that he was conceited or anything. It was just a fact of life that he'd had to get used to. Even before he became famous, girls threw themselves at him all the time because of his looks. But once fame came into play, looks was just the start. Now it was his money or what he could do for their careers that had them flocking in droves. Being around Sunny was just…easy.

Grabbing his phone, he called up Sunny's number. "Hey, Sweet Girl. I'm outside", he said after she picked up.

"Okay. Walking out now." Her voice trembled softly. Gabe knew he had a tough job of making her feel at ease today.

He got out of his old refurbished classic pickup truck in the original green and made his way to the passenger side, so he'd be there to open the truck door for her.

Sunny appeared in the doorway of her building. Gabe took in the sight of her as she stepped outside into the sunlight. His breath caught, his heart pounded, and his palms started to sweat. She was stunning, as usual. Her hair was swept up with her curls in sexy disarray piled atop her head, with a few wispy tendrils that lay gently against her neck, forehead, and temples. She wore a long sheer sundress that nearly touched the ground with a nude lining that stopped at her knees. It had an abstract tropical design on it in neutral as well as vibrant colors intermingled together, that made her skin tone glow. And of course it was cut deep showing off a good portion of her breasts, which would torture him throughout the date. She held the dress up slightly on one side to make sure that she didn't step on the hem. Revealing sexy ankle bands in colorful stones that on closer inspection he realized were part of her deceptively plain flat sandals. And her makeup was minimal. Just enough to highlight her almond shaped eyes and sparkly lip-gloss to emphasize her pouty lips. He thought she definitely knew how to pull off comfortable, elegant, and sexy as hell, all at the same time. She took his breath away.

As she reached him he breathed in her fresh light flowery scent that matched her perfectly. *Sunshine and breezes.* Her face lit up as she scanned the truck. "This is yours?"

"Yep. A 1951 *Chevy 3100*." He rubbed the hood lovingly.

"It's beautiful! I love old cars and trucks. I've always wanted an old truck."

"Do you want to know what is really beautiful?" He paused for emphasis. "You."

She looked down at the ground bashfully. Her cheeks turned

a pretty pink. "Thank you, Gabriel. You look really handsome. What you do for a t-shirt should be illegal."

Now it was his turn to blush. *I'm a thirty-seven year old man, and this woman has me blushing like a schoolboy.* "Thank you, Madison." She smiled at the use of her given name. And with a flourish and a bow, he opened the passenger door. "Your chariot awaits, milady."

~~~

Sunny giggled like a schoolgirl as she slid into the truck. When she had stepped out of her apartment and saw him leaning against the old truck, looking as if he was one of the bad boys that had literally stepped off the pages of one of the hundreds of romance novels she'd buried herself in, she had nearly gone cross-eyed at the sight. The plain white tee could barely contain the muscles that rippled across his shoulders, arms and chest. Even now as she watched him shift and steer through traffic, the muscles in his arms flexed gracefully. His forearms were thick and corded, with huge veins snaking under his skin and a light dusting of black hair. She wondered if it was unusual to want to lick someone's forearms. *I mean…seriously!!! There is no way on this God's green earth that this man could really find me attractive! This shit just doesn't happen in real life. No. Absolutely. NOT!*

Pulling her mind out of bewilderment, she realized that he'd flustered her so much the past couple of days that she hadn't asked him one thing about himself or his new movie. Sure she had read about him in magazines, but who knew what information was real or not. It was time to learn straight from the source.

"So most of our conversations have been about me and I think it's time we changed that. If that's alright with you? I'm sure being in the lime-light you don't want everyone to know your business. But-"

"It's fine Sunny. Ask me whatever you want. I trust you."

Gabe glanced over at her, giving her a warm reassuring smile.

"Well, what is the new movie that you've been filming here?" She said, starting out with a light subject.

"That's an easy one. It's called Redemption. It's about a man, a banker that has been cheating on his wife and just generally ignoring his family. Then a group of bank robbers decide to hold him and his family hostage, forcing him to help them rob his bank. In the meantime, he is also forced to realize just how much he loves his family. And tries to redeem himself, by doing everything in his power to protect his family. That about sums it up. Drama, action and a little bit of romance." Gabe glanced at her to gauge her reaction.

"Nice, it looks like I better clear my calendar for the release, because it sounds like something I'd definitely go see. The description has the earmarks of an *Oscar* and *Golden Globe* nominated film. If the script is well written. Which I can't see you working on anything less than an amazing script." Sunny said matter-of-factly.

"Wow! You really are a movie-buff." Gabe looked at her with a seriously impressed smirk.

"I just love movies. Always have. And for some reason most movie information, even if I've only heard it once, somehow gets stuck in my head. Now ask me about politics, and I've got nothin'." Sunny shrugged, unashamed.

"No worries. I'd rather talk to you about movies than politics. Besides, movies are a safer subject for first dates, anyway." Gabe remarked sensibly.

"That's true. So we'll be sure to also steer clear of religion, Pro-Life/Pro-Choice, and exes. I think that about covers all the first date 'no fly zone' discussions." The more they talked the more Sunny started to relax, like last night when he had successfully cheered her up after the Trent fiasco.

"Yep. I think you got them all. So speaking of movie release dates, I'd love to take you to the premiere of my new movie Clutch, that's coming out in two weeks."

Well, there went her relaxed feeling. "You mean the public,

L.A., red carpet and paparazzi kind of movie premiere?" Sunny closed her eyes, and started to inhale and exhale slowly, trying to control the panic attack she felt coming on.

"Yes, Sunny. A premiere with all the bells and whistles. You also forgot designer dresses, stylists and makeup artists. You know, stuff that ladies seem to like." Gabe mistakenly generalized.

She gave him the stink-eye, unlike he'd ever gotten before. "Do I look like a woman that enjoys all that stuff?"

"Well no. You're charmingly undemanding. But don't you like the idea of being pampered every now and again?" Gabe said, trying to backpedal a little.

"Of course. But I don't have money for all of that, Gabe." Sunny admitted.

"Did I say that you needed to spend any money? It would be on me, as a 'thank you' for keeping me company, during what would be a normally dull night." Gabe persisted.

"I just don't know if I'd feel comfortable being put under a microscope because I'm on the arm of the 'The World's Sexiest Man'." *And I'm found lacking.* She kept that thought to herself.

"Well, you don't have to give me an answer right now. Just think about it." Gabe said, hopeful.

"Okay."

"And Sunny?"

"Yes?"

"I would be honored and the 'The World's *Luckiest* Man' if you accompanied me to the premiere." Sincerity was written all over his face when he glanced at her. *Swoon!*

"Thanks, Gabe. And thank you for being so sweet and patient with me. I may not understand it, but I appreciate it." Sunny stared down at her hands that were wringing in her lap self-consciously.

Gabe reached over and grabbed her left hand, caressing it gently trying to calm her nerves. Unfortunately, it had a different effect than he intended, she was sure. Not until this moment, did she realize that her hands were quite obviously one of her erogenous zones. His fingertips danced and caressed lightly along the back of her hand, her palm and between her fingers. Her body instantly burst into flames, skin flushed and goosebumps raised. Her mouth reflexively opened, her eyes closed and a soft gasp passed her lips. It felt like she had two hearts, one beating through her chest and the other pounding a violent pulse in her clit, making her entire core clench and her thighs squeeze shut. She was literally having tiny orgasms that were sending electric shocks to the pleasure section of her brain. It was the most erotic moment of her life, which was taking place in broad daylight on the freeway.

~~~

Holy FUCK! Sunny's reaction from his simple caress had him nearly coming in his pants. It took every ounce of his concentration not to ruin his jeans before their date even began. Or crash the truck. Hearing her little gasps of pleasure was sending him over the edge. She was so responsive. He couldn't imagine what she'd be like if he actually did something sexual.

"Shit Sunny! You're fucking killin' me here." His jaw was clenching and unclenching as he pulled his hand away. Putting both hands on the steering wheel, trying hard to maintain control, his knuckles turned white from the effort.

Gabe looked over at Sunny and her head was back with her hands covering her face like she was embarrassed. He reached over to pull her hands down from her face, but stopped midway, thinking that touching her again would be a bad idea. He'd be pulling off to the side of the road, laying her across the bench seat, spreading her thick thighs and thrusting into her in ten seconds flat.

"Sunny, please don't be embarrassed by your honest response to my touch. It was beautiful. And the most raw and arousing thing I've ever experienced."

Sunny slowly removed her hands from her face. "Really?"

"Fuck yeah! Can't you tell?" Gabe glanced down at his

apparent erection that even his jeans couldn't hide.

She took a sharply indrawn breath when she followed his gaze down to his lap. "Oh." She softly whispered. "I'm sorry if I've made you uncomfortable."

"Sunny, if you don't stop apologizing I'm seriously going to put you over my knee. I like the things you say, the things you do. I just *like* you. So when you apologize for being you, it pisses me off. So please stop."

"Okay. I won't do it again." Her back straightened and her chin came up imperceptibly. *Good girl.* Gabe wanted. No needed her to understand how amazing she was. Otherwise he was terrified what the media would do to her. He just hoped that he would have enough time to build something strong with her before the world started to interfere. And he knew they would.

To ease the tension that had built between them, Gabe tried to lighten the mood. "Hey why don't you turn on the radio? Pick whatever station you want. And I promise I'll sing whatever song you want me to."

A huge smile spread across her face. "Deal."

~~~

Sunny reached over turning on the old original 1951 car radio. She turned to a station that played the eighties, nineties and today. *Take On Me* by A-ha was playing. She turned to look at Gabe with one raised sassy eyebrow.

"Aw, this song is too high for me!"

"You said any song I wanted." He gave her a sad puppy dog look. "Alright fine. I'll sing with you."

"Okay." A big grin spread across his face.

By this time the song was at the chorus. Perfect. With the windows down, wind whipping their hair they sang at the top of their lungs.

They laughed at how horrible they sounded. Sunny knew not many could pull off those high notes. But it was one of the best classics to sing badly with nothing but pure joy.

By the time the song was over they were relaxed once more, enjoying each other's company. Heading south from the 405 to the 5, singing any and every song that came on the radio whether they knew it or not, making up words if they didn't. Sunny realized they must be headed to San Diego. Or Tijuana. But she didn't think a show involving a stripper and a donkey would make for a good first date. She couldn't possibly guess what he had planned, but she knew it would be great considering how attentive and thoughtful he was towards her.

"Okay Sunny. I want you to close your eyes. Cover them with your hands if you have to, but I don't want you to see where we're going yet.

"Fine." Sunny grumbled with building excitement.

They must have driven about fifteen more minutes before he told her to open her eyes. When she uncovered her eyes, the big sign in front of her filled her with instant joy.

"Sea World! I've never been, but always wanted to go! How did you know?" Sunny was literally bouncing in her seat with anticipation.

"I had no idea. But it just seemed like something fun that you would like." Gabe's grin screamed happy and proud for making the right decision.

"When I was a kid I wanted to work here. I wanted to be a marine biologist. And well, also a veterinarian, a zoologist, and an astronomer. I had some pretty big aspirations back then. And the inability to focus, obviously." She shrugged sheepishly.

Gabe laughed as he got out of the truck, making his way around to open her door. "Come on, Sweet Girl. Let's go meet the fishy co-workers you would've had if you worked here.

"Ha! Funny." Sunny rolled her eyes, but smiled happily. Taking the hand he extended to her, they made their way to the entrance.

Chapter 6

The afternoon spent with Sunny, was one of the most enchanting Gabe could ever remember having. She was just a happy person, filled with joy. It was infectious. He also couldn't ever remember smiling this hard either. His cheeks were killing him. He had no idea how she could smile this much without her face cramping. *Maybe that's why her cheeks are so big and rosy...they've been worked out a lot.* At one point he even had to ask her. She simply replied, "I'm used to it. Though they do ache a little today." She even tried to smoosh down her cheeks with her hands and made a funny face to relax her mouth. But the instant she released her cheeks, the smile bounced right back into place. She just shrugged her shoulders as if to say, 'oh well', and skipped off to the next exhibit. *Adorable.*

That's how the afternoon went; her skipping, zigzagging, or dancing her way from one spot to another, filled with pent up energy. Gabe noticed that if there was music playing, Sunny would invariably start to dance and sing. And people loved it...loved her. They would either dance and sing with her or smile and laugh at the entertainment.

Gabe also realized that Sunny made friends everywhere she went. She wasn't afraid to talk to anyone. She would chitchat in the lines for rides, in front of the sea turtle tank and even while waiting in line to get giant pretzels and frozen lemonade. People just gravitated towards her. He didn't have to worry much about people recognizing him. All the focus was on Sunny. Even the sea mammals loved her.

The best was watching her during the Dolphin Encounter.

The dolphin she interacted with, Phineas, took to her and vice-versa. The trainer had her feed the dolphin fish, made him twirl jump and at the end kissed her on the lips with his long bottle-nose, making Gabe's heart burst. The dolphin even tried to follow her as she walked around the tank as they started to exit the dolphin arena. She looked up at Gabe with a huge grin on her face. He stopped her and wrapped his arms around her shoulders.

"You know, I don't think it's fair that a dolphin got to kiss you before I did." The dolphin had actually given him the perfect lead-in. Hey, he took what he could get.

"Welllll, then I guess there is just one thing that can make it right." Sunny raised her chin, putting her lips in direct line with his.

Gabe slowly bent down and gently brushed his lips across hers, trying to savor the moment. Electric pulses shot through his body and he started to deepen the kiss. *SWOOSH!* Gabe was splashed with a shit ton of water. *What the hell!* Gabe turned and looked to see a dolphin tail dip back into the water. Then the dolphin's head popped up and started squealing, in what suspiciously sounded like a laugh. The trainer had to call the dolphin back and she came over apologizing profusely and directed them towards a locker room with hairdryers he could use to dry himself off.

Sunny had been extra quiet since the incident started. As they walked into the locker room, Gabe looked down at her and saw that she was squeezing her lips together in an attempt to keep from laughing. But failed the instant he looked at her.

"AAAAAAhahahahaha!" She doubled over, clutching her stomach as she laughed at him.

"Humph…" Gabe frowned at her.

This of course, made her laugh harder. "That had to be the cutest thing I think I've ever seen. A jealous dolphin. Hahahahaha!" Gasping, she could barely breathe from laughing so hard.

I'll give you something to gasp about. Gabe thought it was time for him to take a stand for his pride. He took his hat off and threw it onto the counter. Smirking at her, he brought his arms up, reached behind his back, grabbed his t-shirt near the nape of his neck, and slowly started to pull the shirt up. The laughter died quickly as Sunny stared at him with huge eyes, realizing what he was about to do.

~~~

Oh, boy! Sunny gulped. She watched as Gabe lifted his soaking wet t-shirt up from the back. The situation had been so comical that she hadn't noticed how the wet shirt looked transparent and clung to him like a second skin. She noticed now. *Drumroll, please! And the winner of the Hot Guy Wet T-shirt Contest is...*

The shirt came over his head and he also tossed that on the counter with his hat. Then he reached behind her to a rack of towels she hadn't noticed before, his skin and scent so close to her, she thought she might pass out. He grabbed a towel and started rubbing it down he chiseled pecs and washboard abs. *Oh, unfair!* Her hands flexed at her sides with the need to touch him. But she couldn't move. Didn't dare move. But her eyes roved over his body hungrily. Taking in the wide breadth of his chest that tapered down to his sculpted waist.

"Sunny?" His deep voice caressed her like a warm breeze.

She couldn't speak. All she could do was look up into his eyes, which got her every time with that vibrant blue gaze.

"Why haven't you ever touched me? I'm always finding little ways to touch you. Sunny, I *need* you to touch me. I crave your sweetness." Sunny saw that he meant every word, the look in his eyes so vulnerable. And she realized that she'd went out of her way not to touch him, for fear that this would all just be a dream and he'd vanish before her eyes.

Digging deep to find the courage that she needed, she took the few steps that brought her an inch away from his skin. Close enough that if she inhaled deeply her breasts would rub against his stomach. Slowly she reached up and gently placed her fingertips on the scruff that covered his cut jawline. With fingers splayed, she brushed her thumbs along his cheeks. His eyes fluttered closed and nostrils flared. Sunny slid her hands away from his face and focused on his ridiculously broad chest. Her hands rested lightly on his pecs, feeling the dusting of black hairs there. They were springy but soft, tickling her fingers. She then bit her bottom lip as smoothed her hands over the taut skin until her fingers brushed his flat pink nipples. And something in him snapped.

A growl escaped his lips, and before she could process what was happening, he bent down, crushed his lips to hers and wrapped his arms around her lush bottom and lifted her like she weighed nothing. *Holy shit! He can lift me!* She wrapped her legs around his waist as he quickly walked her to the counter, setting her on the edge, biting, nibbling and making a meal of her lips. He pulled back, sharp blue eyes searching warm honey, seeking permission. Getting the answer he needed, his hands grabbed her face and his lips swooped down, tongue plunging into her awaiting mouth.

Once she had touched him, it was like she couldn't stop. Her hands were all over him; his back, shoulders, chest, tight abs, bulging arms and beautiful face. She couldn't get enough of his hot flesh. As their tongues intertwined, mimicking what their bodies wanted to do, Sunny tried to get closer to him, her wet heat seeking his hot steel. But her dress was in the way, tangled around her knees and thighs. Gabe realized what she was trying to do, and brought her arms around his neck and just as politely as he pleased grabbed her butt to lift her up and slid her dress up until it was bunched at her hips, then he sat her back down. Gripping her hips, he slid her closer to the edge of the counter. Her knees spread of their own accord to make room for him in the middle. Her wet panties exposed, she could smell the musky scent of her arousal in the space between them.

"Ah God! I can smell you. Smell how much you want me." Gabe's forehead rested against her shoulder as he breathed in deep. He grasped her hips again pulling her up against an impressive (as far as she could tell), erection encased in denim. Little gasps slipped through her lips every time he thrust forward, rubbing his hardness against her covered clit, the friction causing delicious need to slice through her. Until her gasps became cries, becoming louder and more frequent. She felt the climax building as he pressed soft kisses all over her face, continuing to grind into her. And as she went over the edge, he covered her mouth in a heated kiss, tongues stroking absorbing her loud cry.

Sunny reluctantly broke the kiss and Gabe rested his forehead against hers, their breath mixing harsh and hot. Never had she found her orgasm with a man, and this man quickly brought one out just from *dry-humping* her!

"And that is exactly why I hadn't touched you. I knew I'd have no control." Sunny whispered.

"Hmm…," Gabe had no words yet. He just rubbed his hardness against her once, twice, three times. Sunny shuddered, her clit still sensitive. Gabe finally pulled away slowly, putting needed distance between them. He tried to adjust himself in the crotch area to get more comfortable, but Sunny could see the strain on his jeans and his face.

"Oh God, Gabe! I'm so sorry to keep doing this to you. I'm gonna end up giving you blue balls." Sunny cringed seeing the discomfort on his face.

"Sunny-" Gabe said in warning.

"Wait." Sunny interrupted. "Before you yell at me. I wasn't apologizing for being me, I was apologizing for putting you through pain. I don't want to see you suffer because you're giving me so much pleasure and you're getting none in return." She reached across and grabbed him by the belt and pulled him closer once more. With trembling fingers she unbuckled his belt, unbuttoned his jeans and was sliding down the zipper when they heard someone enter the locker room.

Sunny quickly jumped down from the counter, straightening her dress. While Gabe zipped back up, fastened his belt and picked up his shirt and the hairdryer and started drying it, right as the trainer from earlier came around the corner.

"Hey guys. How's it coming along?" Gabe turned slightly away from her and looked down, apparently not wanting her to recognize him.

Sunny stepped up. "Oh, we're doing good. Almost finished."

"Yeah, sorry again. Phineas doesn't normally do things like that. He must have really liked you." She said smiling at Sunny.

"I guess so. It was sweet though."

"Pfft!" That came from Gabe's general direction and Sunny had to laugh to herself. *Jealous much...over a dolphin!*

"Well, I better get back. Have a good evening. And take as long as you need." She waved goodbye as she walked around the corner.

Sunny walked up to Gabe's back, wrapped her arms around his waist, pressed her nose against his firm but soft skin and rubbed her face back and forth against him. His body tensed with pent up need. Sunny spoke against his back, "Maybe I'll finish up what I started, later." Gabe just put his head back and a groan came from deep in his chest. It rumbled so deep she could feel it through his back.

"You're gonna be the death of me, woman." His voice came out in a thick sexy rasp.

Sunny just smiled into his back and squeezed him a little harder.

"Alright, Sweet Girl. Let me get you out of here before I take advantage of you in a bathroom stall." He pulled her around to his front to give her a big hug, before he slipped back on his shirt and hat. Grabbing her hand, they headed out.

Chapter 7

They walked back to his truck hand in hand. Once there he unlocked and opened the passenger door for her to get in. She had never been so spoiled before. She knew that she had told him she deserved better than 'booty-call' treatment, but actually getting what you want, she realized would take some getting used to.

Gabe opened the driver side door and reached back to grab a shirt that had been hanging behind the seat. "Give me just a second." He smiled at her while he shrugged on a beautiful azure blue dress shirt with shiny pinstripes of the same color, over his now dry t-shirt. The color of the shirt seemed to make his eyes glimmer like a wolf's. All predator and she was his prey. He then pulled dress shoes and socks out of a gym bag that was tucked under the seat. He pulled off his gym shoes and gym socks and swapped them out for the dressy replacements. He took off his hat and grabbing one of the bottles of water he had purchased earlier for them, he took the cap off, poured some in his hands and slid his wet hands through his hair. Sunny realized he was rewetting his wavy locks to get rid of his 'hat-hair'.

She was enthralled at the entire process of him changing for a night out. "Well my, my, my." Sunny said as she fanned herself with her hand.

Gabe looked up from his reflection after fixing his hair and gave Sunny a cocky grin. "Is there something you like?"

"Hell yes!"

Gabe got into the truck, leaned across and kissed Sunny quickly but deeply on the lips, just a hint of his tongue flicking her lips. Now that the first kiss was over with, Sunny knew it was game on. There would be constant stolen kisses from here on out.

"So you've decided to ditch the hat? Isn't that a little risky? People are going to recognize you instantly. You're kinda hard to ignore." Sunny looked him up and down as he started the truck and pulled out of the parking lot.

"I know. But a lot of the dress codes for the bars and clubs are strict. And besides, I've hung out around here a lot and no one bothers me too much. It's nice." Gabe reached over and squeezed Sunny's hand reassuringly.

She looked down at their hands, her heart warming. "Okay, I trust your judgment. I just don't want a repeat of last night. That was pretty awful."

"Yeah it was. I got my ass pinched and grabbed several times. And a couple of girls and quite possibly even a dude cupped my junk!"

"Ha! How do you know it was a guy?" Sunny laughed skeptically.

"Because if it wasn't, that chick had awfully big hands." His face was dead serious.

Sunny's head fell onto his shoulder as she laughed hysterically. Shaking her head back and forth on his shoulder, she wiped the tears off her face. She leaned a bit closer and kissed him on the cheek, finding it easier and easier to show her affection towards him without the fear of being rejected.

"Just to let you know, I told Trent last night that I quit."

"What? Oh Sunny, I never intended for that to happen. I know how much you love to perform, I could tell." Gabe smoothed a tendril away from her cheek and looked down at her sadly.

"It's okay. I can always find someone else that can play a guitar and willing to sing in front of a crowd. Don't worry about it." She covered the hand he still had on her face comfortingly.

"So are you hungry?"

"Yeah, a little."

"Well I'm starving…and not for food." He stared down at

her lips. Then a horn honked behind them, making them jump apart, letting them know that the light they were stopped at had turned green. He blew out a harsh breath. "Alright, let's go eat...food."

<p style="text-align:center">~~~</p>

Gabe parked on a side street in Mission Beach, an area filled with bars, restaurants, shops and a boardwalk amusement park. Laid-back and chill enough for Sunny to feel comfortable and at ease. Their first stop would be Risqué, an intimate lounge with good food.

They walked the few blocks to the lounge, hand in hand. He was glad that she was becoming comfortable enough to show and reciprocate affection. He was also glad that it was now evening, dark enough for people not to recognize him. Plus, most people didn't usually expect to see anyone famous walking down the street. He wasn't ready for his date to be interrupted, things were going too well. And Sunny deserved his full attention.

When they got to the door, they were instantly let in without question. Gabe knew the bouncer from the previous times he had come to the lounge. Walking in, the lounge had a dark seductive feel to it. It was decorated in black, red, silver and gold. With leather booths and velvet couches. They sat next to each other on one of the cozy leather love seats. Across the room from where they sat were works of art of the naked female form, many similar to the Renaissance age, where the women reminded him of Sunny. Soft with dangerous curves, like what he felt a woman should look like.

As he looked at Sunny, who was looking around taking in the details of the place, he thought of the women he'd been with in the past. Several had been hard-bodies, with hours spent at the gym. Others skinny and waif-like, that ate like rabbits. But gazing at Sunny he realized that none of that was as appealing as her plush and inviting curves. He just wanted to bury himself in her and not leave for a week. If only he could convince her of this, he'd be in business.

A waitress walked up to take their food and drink orders. Her mouth dropped open when she realized who he was. "Wow. Mr. Wolf, my name is Bree and I'll be your server tonight. And if there is anything you need, I mean anything, don't hesitate to ask. Is there anything I can get you started with?"

Gabe recognized the innuendo in her voice. But there was absolutely nothing that the frail, bleach blonde with gigantic fake boobs could do for him. Noticing that she hadn't even acknowledged Sunny's presence, Gabe looked to Sunny to place her order first. "Ladies first." He pointedly looked at Bree then at Sunny, letting her know that he was in fact with the beautiful girl next to him. "What would you like to drink, Sweet Girl?"

For the second time the waitress's mouth dropped open and gave Sunny a look he didn't appreciate. "Oh, sorry. What can I get for you?" She asked in a snotty tone.

Sunny ignored her and gave Gabe an innocent look. "I'll take a *Corona*, with lime and a salt shaker please."

Gabe looked at Sunny suspiciously, wondering what she was up too. "I'll take a whiskey, neat."

The waitress scurried away to grab their orders. Gabe continued stared at Sunny curiously.

"What?"

"You're up to something."

"I have no idea what you're talking about." She smiled sweetly at him as the waitress brought their drinks. She placed their drinks in front of them, as well as Sunny's salt shaker and lime on a napkin.

"Would you also like to order something to eat?" The waitress asked.

"Give us a few minutes, thank you." Gabe responded not looking at her, but focused on Sunny to see what she planned to do with the lime and salt. He understood the lime, but had no idea what the salt could be for.

Sunny grabbed the lime, squeezed the juices into the bottle of *Corona*, took the lime and rubbed it all over the neck of the bottle, coating the neck in lime juice. Then she grabbed the bottle tilted it to the side, took the salt shaker and started to shake salt onto the bottleneck as she rotated it, until the neck was lightly covered in salt. *What the hell is she doing? OH. MY. GOD!*

Gabe watched as she brought the bottle to her mouth, then placed her tongue on the bottom of the neck, slowly licked up to the top and then tipped the bottle up taking a sip of the beer. She placed the bottle back on the table and looked up at him from under her lashes coyly. She was the only woman who could make him go from normal to rock hard in the span of a second.

"You totally did that on purpose!" Gabe exclaimed.

"I did not! I love *Corona* and that is how I was taught to drink it the first time I ever had one." Sunny defended.

"Right. You could've had any of the many beers they have here. Even your favorite 'blue mountains', but you decide to get the beer that you happen to lick like a champ? I really think that you are trying to kill me. Death by exploding blue balls!" He scowled at her.

"Well since you put it that way, now I just feel bad. I didn't mean to get you worked up. Well not *that* worked up."

Gabe leaned into her, burying his nose in her neck and rubbing it up to her ear. "Don't worry I have every intention of getting you back later. Much. Much. Later." Each of the last words were punctuated by a kiss on her ear, finished by a quick flick of his tongue on the shell. Uncontrollable shivers coursed through her body.

"Ahem." A voice broke into their playful flirtation. They looked up to see the sour faced waitress. "Are you ready to place your orders?"

"Oh, sorry. I may not be that hungry anymore, seeing as how good she tastes." Gabe purposely said it to piss *Barbie* off.

"Don't listen to him. Sorry, we haven't even looked at the menu. Hold on just as sec." Sunny quickly scanned the menu. "Hey Gabe, do you like hummus?"

"Love it."

"Okay, we'll start with the hummus platter appetizer. And

I'll have the Mediterranean Stromboli."

"And I'll get the Buffalo Chicken Stromboli. Thank you." Gabe ordered and quickly dismissed the waitress. Turning back to Sunny, "So, you have a thing for Mediterranean cuisine?"

"Yeah. Most of it is light and flavorful. I love it."

Hmm...maybe one day, if everything goes the way I hope it will, I'll take her there.

"You're flavorful." Gabe murmured while he reached over to nibble on her neck and shoulder.

"And you're full of it." Sunny said breathlessly as she pushed him off of her neck. "So I only got to ask you one question about yourself earlier. That wasn't nearly enough."

Gabe pretended to pout at not being able to taste more of her skin, but it was probably a good idea that she stopped him, because he knew he couldn't. "Alright shoot."

"Well, first let me start by saying that *IMDB* is one of my favorite websites and apps of all time. I'm looking up movie and actor information almost on a daily basis. So yes, I have looked you up before. But I'm not a stalker or anything." She was looking down at her wringing hands again.

Gabe touched her chin with his index finger and pressed up, forcing her to look at him. "No one would accuse you of being a stalker, Sweet Girl. Most times you're trying to run away from me."

"True. Though I'm trying to stay put."

"I've noticed. And I'm glad." He leaned forward and gently placed a kiss on her ridiculously soft lips and had to restrain himself from going deeper.

Again, she pulled back and inhaled and exhaled slowly. As if, she was trying to check herself as well. "So as I was saying. I noticed that your Mini Biography was empty, but there was some Trivia about you. One of the things it said was that you were an orphan. And I've seen interviews with you, where they asked you questions about your childhood, but you always find a way to dodge the questions. So...what was your childhood like?" She finally asked hesitantly.

This subject he had always avoided like the plague. His past life was no one's business. And his skin usually prickled in anger when anyone asked about it. But now, he felt like purging himself. Telling her everything. He realized that he trusted her…that much. With his past. *With my heart. Shit!*

He knew he was in trouble now, if she walked away. If she decided that she couldn't deal with the constant scrutiny of being with someone in the spotlight. And she walked away. She'd be taking all of him with her. That's just how much she had already gotten under his skin. Infiltrated his every emotion. Now that he knew her and she was a part of his life, he couldn't imagine her not being in it. *How could this beautiful tiny curvy little spitfire come to mean so much to me in only three days' time?* He couldn't figure it out, but decided not to question it. And to just open up. *Well, here goes nothing.* And for the first time since he had become *Gabriel Wolf* the actor, he told his story.

Gabe cleared his throat, "Sunny, you have to understand that this is hard for me. I've never talked about my past with anyone before." He took a deep breath, fortifying himself to tell a difficult part of his life. And gaining strength from the reassuring and attentive look she gave him. But before he could start the waitress came back with their appetizer. She left quickly after placing the plates on the table, sensing the tension.

Sunny picked up some of the warm pita bread and dipped it into the hummus, patiently waiting for him to begin. He loved that she wasn't pushing, just giving him time to get his thoughts together. As if she had all the time in the world.

~~~

He also took some food, chewed thoughtfully and began again. "*IMDB* was right. I was…am an orphan." Sunny could see the hurt written all over his face when he said the word 'orphan'. It broke her heart. He continued through the pain. "I was abandoned at the hospital after I was born. My mother left a note, a picture, and a baby blanket that she had crocheted herself. In the note she wrote that her and my father had been happily married. Her name was Francesca and she was from Spain...Mataró, a coastal city outside of Barcelona. And my father Erik Wolf was from Oslo, Norway. I guess he came from a wealthy family that wanted him to follow his in father's and grandfather's footsteps and become a doctor. And before he went off to medical school, he took a holiday, traveling around Europe. That's when he met my mother. She was eighteen and he was twenty-two.

"They fell in love, though my mother's family had hand-picked a Spanish boy they wanted her to marry and didn't want her to have anything to do with my dad. And I guess my dad's family was pressuring him to come back to start medical school, also disapproving of his Spanish sweetheart. So he took what money he could get from his trust fund and they ran off to America. He was able to obtain a scholarship at the *University of Michigan*. So they moved there and she got jobs cleaning houses, while he went to school. She got pregnant, so they decided to get married at the courthouse. When she went into labor, he was in class, so a neighbor they had made friends with, drove her to the hospital. On his way to the hospital, my father was rushing and not paying attention, when a car struck him while he was crossing the street." Sunny gasped, not realizing that the story would have such a tragic turn to it.

"He didn't make it. But I guess he got to see me once, before he died. My mother was distraught and didn't know how she would make it in this country without him. So her friend helped her get enough money to make it back to Spain. And she left me in the hopes that I would have better opportunities and a better life here. She left the note, a picture of her and my father and the blanket on her hospital bed, before she snuck out." Gabe rubbed his hands over his face, through his hair and then starting fiddling with his empty glass. He looked so incredibly sad and remote. With the need to touch him, soothe him, Sunny reached over and clutched his hand. Giving it a firm squeeze.

Their bitch of a waitress came over to drop off their food and more drinks. Sunny could tell that she noticed the tension and their serious faces, and guessing wrong at the cause, because she gave a satisfied smile thinking that they were fighting or something. And she walked away, swaying her sad excuse for hips, as if Gabe would notice. But he was too deep in thought, to pay her much attention. Sunny wasn't even sure if he realized that his food was now in front of him.

"You don't have to go on if you don't want to." Sunny stroked his shoulder and back.

"No it's okay. I want to tell you." He blew out a breath making his cheeks puff out. "So as you can guess, like so many stories, I got lost in the system. I didn't get adopted before I passed the cute baby stage. Then that's when I got passed around from foster home to foster home. Some were better than others. Because I was a cute kid the foster mothers loved me. But that only pissed off the other foster kids, and they would find ways to pinch, hit or kick me when no one was looking.

"When I got older, I grew fast, and looked so much older than most of the other boys my age. The foster mothers noticed that too. And so did the foster fathers. My first time was with a foster mother. When her husband found out, he beat the shit outta me. And then I was sent off to the next foster home. This happened a lot. Either the husbands would send me packing before his wife could even think about getting to me or they would kick my ass when she did. I learned to defend myself pretty quickly and used gym class to bulk up and get stronger. But I think Child Services finally wised up and I was sent to a foster home where the parents were actually more like grandparents, so they were fine with me and virtually drama free. Though, I was already almost seventeen by that time. So I only had about a year and a half before I was out of the system and on my own.

"That was when I found my passion. I was angry all the time. And the drama teacher noticed me and said that I could direct all my frustrations into acting. I got involved in the spring play and loved it. Was good at it. That's when I got the idea to move to L.A. I found any jobs that I could get in order to save up enough money to buy a bus ticket. And I did. I graduated by the skin of my teeth in June and spent the next two months busting my ass. And when I turned eighteen that August, I was up and ready to go. Packed up the few clothes I had, my mother's note, picture and blanket and got on a bus.

"When I arrived in L.A., I worked as a waiter, of course, and stayed at a shelter because I didn't have enough money for an apartment yet. I saw in the paper that they were casting extras for a movie. So I went and people involved in the movie noticed me, I guess I stood out, and that was it. They set me up with an agent and I was cast in my first speaking role in a movie a month later. And it's been chaos ever since." He took a deep inhalation of air and blew it out quickly. Like finally getting it off his chest released something inside of him.

Sunny realized how crazy his life must feel to him. Going from feeling like absolutely no one wanted him to everyone wanting him in an instant. And not necessarily wanting him for who he was, but for his status. That had to be a little confusing. Technically, he had never been wanted or loved for who he truly was. *Well I plan on changing that right now!*

"Have you ever tried to find your mother?"

"No." The word was said sharply. *Uh oh, dangerous territory. Thread lightly.*

"Why not? She obviously loved you. Wanted a better life for you. She probably didn't think you would ever suffer the way you did." Sunny said gently.

"I said no. She was weak. She left me, apparently didn't love me enough and left me to have one hell of a childhood. She gave me a name and a few mementos. Great. I have nothing to say to her. And that's final." Gabe grabbed a knife and fork, cutting into his food angrily.

Sunny knew that she had crossed the line, but she felt she had to try. For his sake, and the sake of his mother, whom she was sure loved him deeply. She quietly started eating as well, staying silent to give him some space.

Gabe startled her, when he suddenly grabbed her hand in a vise-like grip. Her head quickly turned to look at him. He let go of her hand to envelope her face with his large hands. He looked at her with a kind of desperation.

"I'm so sorry, Sunny. I didn't mean to take out my anger on you. I just get so…I don't know. Just please forgive me." He said fiercely.

"Oh Gabriel, I'm not mad at you. I can understand why you're upset. I shouldn't have pushed you." She paused and placed her hand along his cheek. "I adore you, Gabriel. You're a good man."

He instantly pulled her face to his, devouring her mouth. As if it was the last kiss they'd ever have. Sunny was thankful the lounge was pretty dark. Because she was sure they'd be causing more of a spectacle than they already were.

She pulled back, and with her hands on his face, she kissed his forehead, eyelids, nose, cheeks, strong chin and finally a soft peck on his firm lips. She was making sure she infused every ounce of the love she had to give and that he very much needed into every kiss.

Sunny finally pulled away from him. "Let's finish our food", she said smiling softly at him. He gazed at her with what looked like adoration, which she tried to ignore for fear of hoping for too much.

~~~

Shit. Shit. Shit! He was in love with her. *I am completely head over heels in love with her.* He couldn't fathom how anyone could fall in love with someone after knowing them only a few days. But it was happening. To *him*. And it was scary as hell. He hadn't let anyone in…ever. He had always been afraid of rejection. Of giving his heart to someone completely and risk them walking away when they found him lacking. But even after telling Sunny his story, she still looked at him as if he was anything but lacking. She seemed to accept him for who he really was.

Though he couldn't entirely find fault with the women of his past. He had never given them the chance to know who he really was. Once the relationship got to the point of learning everything about each other, he would always find a way to bail. But Sunny did what she always does best. She saturated herself into his life and heart, like sunshine penetrates through the cracks in concrete.

After they had finished their dinner, Sunny excused herself, and headed to the ladies' room. Gabe watched as she walked away, admiring her form. He shook his head, trying to remove the hazy cloud of sensuality that blanketed him from watching her. That's when he saw the over-inflated stick figure that was their waitress walking towards him. She tried sashaying her hips seductively, and after watching Sunny's curvy hips sway, he found the waitress's walk decidedly deficient.

"Here's your check handsome. And if you're ever interested in someone that is a little better suited for being on your arm, give me a call. My number is on the back of your receipt." She bit the bottom of her unnaturally puffy Botox injected lip.

Gross. Gabe couldn't get over the nerve of this brash, deluded overconfident bimbo. He picked up the receipt with her number on it, inspected it thoughtfully. Then he slowly started tearing it into tiny little pieces in front of her face. Letting the pieces scatter across the table when he was finished, all the while looking right into her eyes.

"'Better suited', huh? And you think *you're* better suited?" Gabe scoffed. "Sweetheart, when I take a woman into my bed, I need to make sure she's got curves to handle my…*size*. Curves you seem to be lacking. And I also don't want to worry that when I squeeze too hard or kiss too roughly that she doesn't pop from her expensive upgrades. I know what I need and want. And you're not it." He reached into his pocket, pulled out his wallet, slid out his credit card and handed it to the dumbfounded waitress. Tears threatened to spill down her over-done face as she stormed away, and behind her stood Sunny.

"Holy shit! What in the world could she have said that made

you say those things to her?" Sunny asked in shock.

Damn. If Gabe didn't tell her, he'd run the risk of her thinking he was a dick to wait staff just for shits and giggles. And if he did, it may hurt her feelings that the girl would think Sunny didn't suit him. *Time to improvise.* "She just tried to give me her number behind your back. It was rude and disrespectful to you and me. I didn't appreciate it, so I put her in her place." He shrugged as if it was nothing.

"I'd say so. Man, I'd hate to be her right now." Sunny cringed.

"You'd never be her, Sweet Girl. You'd never do something as classless as that."

"I would hope not. But sometimes you find people will do desperate things that they thought they'd never do for a chance at something they've always wanted. That includes stepping on others. Unfortunately. I guess I should just be lucky that I've found such a stand-up guy." She gave him a sassy little smirk, making him chuckle.

Another waitress walked over to give Gabe the final receipt to add gratuity and sign. Their actual waitress must have been really upset if she sent someone else. She was nowhere to be seen. Gabe didn't care. What she did was wrong. Normally he gave enormous tips, having been a waiter once upon a time, but this time he gave her the standard twenty percent. No more, no less. She didn't deserve it. And since he'd been there quite a few times in the past and had tipped generously, he was sure she'd hear about it and know that it was how she acted that affected her tip.

"Alright, let's get outta here", he stood up and took Sunny's hand to walk her out.

Once outside, Gabe stopped and took a deep breath of the fresh sea air. It was a beautiful spring night…perfect for a walk.

"I'm not ready to take you home yet." Gabe looked down at Sunny.

"I'm not ready to go home yet." She smiled up at him.

"How about a walk? It's a beautiful night." He suggested.

"That sounds perfect."

Gabe turned and started towards the beach, three blocks away. He had to make sure that he watched his pace. Sunny was so small and his legs took much longer strides than hers, that he'd end up dragging her along if he wasn't paying attention. So he tried to match her small steps.

"Thank you." Sunny said quietly.

He looked over at her confused. "For what?"

"For slowing your pace. I'm shorter than most people and walking with really tall people sucks. I'm always out of breath trying to keep up. My dad is really tall, so I've been trying to keep up for thirty-four years." She looked at him with laughter in her eyes.

"Yeah, I was thinking that very same thing. I was like 'if I walk too fast, I'll end up dragging her'. So I tried slowing it down for you." He winked at her, making her flush.

"Well, it's much appreciated."

"So you're thirty-four? I was wondering, but I know that you're never supposed to ask a woman's age."

"Soon, I turn the big three-five in October. The eighteenth." She informed him.

"Wow. You look good. It was a hard guess. Your maturity says you're in your thirties. But your fun-loving personality and spirit make you seem so much younger. Though I'm really glad you're thirty-five, because you're the perfect age for me."

"Thanks. Yeah, you're thirty-seven, soon to be thirty-eight, right?" She looked up at him sheepishly.

"I know, I know. *IMDB*, right?" Gabe grinned at her, knowing.

She giggled a little, "Yep. That's where I get all my entertainment four-one-one."

Gabe stopped, grabbed her around the waist and lifted her to his level with little effort. "You're a dork…but an adorable one." Then he kissed her soundly on the mouth, before putting her back on her feet.

Staying away from the busy and bright boardwalk, they

made it to the beach, slipping their shoes off before stepping in the sand. The water was an inky black, hard to see in the darkness. Though Gabe could hear it, and the sound was soothing. They walked closer to the water, drawn to it. And Gabe rolled up his jeans when they were near the surf. He watched Sunny lift her dress higher to avoid the tide. The saltwater rushed up to their toes.

"AH!" Sunny screeched and ran away from the water.

"Woo! That's cold!" Gabe shouted. Then before Sunny could get away, he snatched her up from behind and swung her towards the water.

"Ahh! GABE!" He continued to swing her around inching her toes closer and closer to the rushing waves, laughing the whole time. "Gabriel Wolf! DON'T! YOU! DARE! Put me down!" As a wave came up, this time he dipped her legs up to her lower calves in the water. "NOOO! Not in the water, on the sand! You big jerk!"

Finally, he put her down on the sand, grinning at her like the lovesick fool that he was. "You know, you're adorable when you scream like a little girl."

"You're a shithead, you know that?!" She scowled at him, as she playfully smacked at his chest.

"I've been called worse, trust me." He chuckled at her.

"Harrumph. I'm sure."

"Come on, let's go sit down for a little while." He led her over to a lifeguard tower. They climbed up and sat on the top platform. "So you mentioned your dad earlier, I'd love to hear about your family. Your childhood. What makes you...you." Gabe asked inquisitively.

"Well, there's not a whole lot to it. My parents are still together after forty-five years. My mother was an elementary school teacher and my dad worked as a technician for the electric company. Sam and Donna Stone. They're both retired now and live in New Mexico. And I have an older brother, Jace. He's head chef at a nice restaurant in downtown Chicago. And that's my family. And I'm the slacker of the family." Sunny shrugged.

"No you're the baby. No wonder you're so carefree and happy. You've been well loved." She gave him a guilty look. "I know what you're thinking. So stop it. You have nothing to feel guilty over, because you have a loving family. It just gives me hope that it's all possible. Love, family...happiness." Gabe gazed at her, hoping to convey in one look, how much he wanted that with her. *A week ago I couldn't imagine dating one woman exclusively. And now I'm imagining a lifetime with this one.*

"You should believe that it's possible, because it is. And I think you deserve that happiness more than most."

He had to change the subject before she made him cry or something horrible like that. *Jesus!* "So, what else?"

"What do you mean, 'what else'?" Sunny said, scrunching her eyebrows together.

"Tell me stories about your childhood, what made you who you are?" Gabe asked, wanting to know everything about her.

"There's not much to tell. I played outside 'til the streetlights came on, drank from the garden hose, and ran through sprinklers in the summer", she shrugged.

"All of which sounds like perfection. But what made you so shy and self-conscious when it comes to men? You can be so down on yourself, and I just don't get it. You're beautiful."

"Ha." She laughed without real humor. "Maybe you think so, which is strange to me, because most of the time I'm ignored by guys. And it only became worse when I got here, to California. But anyway, I guess it's because I was teased when I was a kid for being chubby. And I just haven't gotten over it.

"I didn't date all throughout high school and college. I was too shy and the guys I liked didn't like me. And the guys that did like me, were way to sexually aggressive for my virgin sensibilities. They scared the crap outta me. It wasn't until I was twenty-two that I lost my virginity, when I met my first love. Who turned out to be a minor klepto. That relationship lasted for a year. And I've only had one more relationship since then. That lasted four years and was a huge waste of time. He was a total commitment-phobe, and strung me along the whole time, claiming that he wanted to marry me. But I guess motorcycles and *Mustangs* were more important than buying a ring. That was four years ago. In the end I'm glad that it didn't work out, because in hindsight, we were *not* a good match. The main thing I regret about that relationship was letting him keep my dog when I moved out here. Oh, and guess what?"

"What?"

"My ex made sure he called me up this past Christmas to let me know that he proposed to his girlfriend of only one year. And he used *my* dog to propose! I swear you can't make this shit up!" Sunny just shook her head.

Gabe was speechless. This girl was amazing, and yet she had been made fun of, ignored or treated like shit. *Thank God!* Gabe realized his good fortune, because in normal circumstances, she'd have been snatched up years ago.

"I'm truly baffled, but so incredibly thankful that none of them realized your worth." Gabe jumped down to the platform that was a few feet below where they were sitting putting them more at eye-level, and stepped between her legs. "You're stunning, and I can't keep my hands off of you."

He brought his hands up to her face and pulled her in for a kiss. He gave her a soft peck, and then slowly brushed his mouth back and forth across her honeyed lips. Gabe's tongue flicked between her lips. Sunny's mouth opened on a sharp inhale and he took advantage of her offering to stroke his tongue deeper into her warm mouth. Their tongues danced together, not able to get enough.

Gabe released her mouth, kissing a trail down her jaw to her neck. Kissing, licking, and biting the sensitive skin there. He moved to her shoulder and the straps of her dress and bra. Reaching up, he pulled down the left side, kissing the skin he bared. Now that the material was loose enough, he tugged down the material of her dress and the lacey cup of her bra to reveal one heavy decadent breast. It was dark chocolate tipped. Her areola was large and the cool air caused her nipple to pucker and harden.

Her chest rose and fell with her labored breaths. Each inhale made her breast rise closer to his mouth. He had to taste her. His tongue flicked against her tender nipple, causing her to cry out. He swirled his tongue around, leaving her skin wet and gleaming. Needing to taste more of her, he sucked her breast into his mouth, trying to get as much of her as he could. Her constant cries were lost to the sounds of the wind and surf.

"You're so beautiful." Gabe said pulling his mouth away from her flesh, then grabbing her face once more to devour her mouth.

Her hands released the death grip she had on the wooden platform and plunged into his hair, her nails scraping against his scalp. She had him on fire. He needed to be inside her, but he knew she wasn't ready. So he did the next best thing, he had to touch her. Sliding her dress up her legs, Sunny adjusted to give him better access. Once the dress was pushed up to her hips, his hand stroked up from her calf to tickle her knee, then up her luscious thighs to the juncture of her legs.

He could feel the heat and dampness radiating off of her through the cotton of her panties. Not able to hold back any longer, he pushed the material to the side and touched her slick opening.

"Aahhh!" Her head thrown back, she cried out and her hips rolled against his hand, trying to get closer.

"Oh God, Sunny! You're so wet." Gabe slid his middle finger inside her snug opening. "And so tight."

"Ah...it...it's been...ahhh!" Sunny stuttered out between pants.

"What, Sweet Girl? 'It's been' what? Gabe breathed the words against her lips.

"...four ye...years. Gabe, please!" She begged.

"Don't worry, I've got you."

He slid another finger in her soft wet walls that gripped his fingers. His fingers crooked forward in the 'come here' motion, connecting with her g-spot. At the very same time his thumb brushed lightly against her clit, once, twice and she detonated.

Quickly Gabe covered her mouth with his as she screamed. Her inner walls flooded with moisture and contracted around his fingers. He milked every last spasm out of her, caressing her gently.

He rested his forehead against Sunny's, "You're the sexiest, most responsive woman that I have ever met. You're breathtaking." He bent his head down to tease her exposed nipple one last time with his tongue. Her breath hitched and her sex fluttered reflexively.

Slowly, reluctantly he slid his fingers from her warmth and brought his hand to his mouth to gently suck the juices from his two fingers. He never took his eyes off her in the process. At this point he was going to explode from lack of release. He had been sporting a massive erection for about three quarters of the date. But the last thing he wanted to do was push her.

Gabe slipped the straps of her bra and dress back into place, restored her panties to their original position and pulled her dress down over her legs.

"And what about you? Don't you deserve some release?" Sunny caressed the bulge in his jeans, then reached for his belt buckle, when a spotlight from a passing police patrol car in the parking lot, swept past them. *Fuck!*

"The beach is now closed. Time to head home folks." A disembodied voice said through a loud speaker. Luckily only part of them could be seen from the parking lot, with the lifeguard tower blocking most of them to the police. But it was still enough to get caught.

Gabe re-buckled his belt. "Seriously! Your poor balls are going to explode at this point!" Sunny looked indignantly at the receding cop car.

"Don't worry about it, Sunny. I'll live. I'll just go home and take a cold shower. Wait, on second thought, maybe I'll take a *hot* shower and think about you the entire time." He winked at Sunny devilishly.

"You are a total scoundrel!" She pushed at him playfully.

"Scoundrel? What am I, a seventeenth century pirate or

something? Have you been reading a lot of romance novels lately?"

"You have no idea. Come on, *Captain Sparrow*, we better get out of here."

Gabe barked out a laugh and grabbed the hand she held out.

Chapter 8

Sunny woke up the next day with the biggest smile possible. She was daydreaming about the previous night, before she realized what had woke her up in the first place. Her cellphone was blaring Buckcherry's *Crazy Bitch*. It was Alyssa.

"Hey." She answered brightly, like she hadn't been asleep just a moment ago.

"Hey? That's all you've got to say? The moment you saw it was me calling, you should have answered, 'yes, he is hung like a horse' or 'hello, he gave me multiple orgasms so good that my toes are still cramped from curling so much'." Alyssa ranted into the phone.

Sunny giggled in response. "Well it wasn't exactly like that, Nasty! I mean I did have a couple of orgasms, but we didn't have sex."

"Wait! What? I need details!" Sunny had to hold the phone away from ear, because of Alyssa's screeching.

"You know…dry humping and hand jobs. That kind of thing. But it was more than that. He was so sweet and attentive. More often than not he was so much more than his status. And I got to see the man he is." Sunny sighed, a goofy grin covering her face.

"I seriously hate you, Sunny!" Alyssa said jokingly. "But as much as I hate you, you really do deserve to be happy. So he better be good to you or I'm gonna kick his tight perfect ass! Now get *your* ass up here. We can have coffee while you tell me everything."

Sunny got up and brushed her teeth before heading upstairs to give Alyssa a recap of the night. She knew she had to edit a little. The things about his private life that he shared with her were not open for discussion. He trusted her and she wanted to keep it that way.

~~~

Gabe found himself smiling like a jackass on set all day. Occasionally, he'd catch himself whistling between takes. *Since when have I ever whistled?*

"You're awfully happy today, Gabe." Jessica his co-star wife commented as she passed him on her way to her trailer.

Gabe just gave a non-committal shrug. "Can't a man have a good day", he smiled.

He liked her well enough, but her tendency towards diva behavior, stopped him from getting to close to her. They had decent chemistry on-screen, but that's where it stopped.

She didn't seem to care enough to stop and question him further, and he was grateful. So while they had this break, he took time out to text Sunny. He would've rather called her, but he wasn't sure whether she was getting ready for work or not.

Gabe: *Good morning, Sweet Girl.*

Sunny: *Good morning, Gabriel. How r u?*

Gabe: *Good. On set. Boring. I'd rather be with you. How r u?*

Sunny: *I'm great. I doubt being on a movie set is boring. Just sitting having coffee with Alyssa. She's badgering me for details. But no worries, ur private life will remain private. Just telling her how sexy u r. ;)*

Gabe: *I trust you. Hmm…how sexy I am? Well, what's the verdict? How sexy am I? :P*

Sunny: *That kind of sexiness can't be measured.*

Gabe: *When can I see you again?*

Sunny: *I don't know. I'm off again Monday. Or maybe if you can get away, we could do lunch before I go to work or dinner after I get off?*

Gabe started to hatch a plan for next weekend.

Gabe: *Hey, try to see if you can get the weekend off. I'd like to spend it with you. We're not filming because of Gay Pride this weekend.*
Sunny: *Ok, I'll see what I can do. But don't get ur hopes up, weekends are hard to come by in retail.*
Gabe: *See what u can do. But call off if they won't give it to u. I'll pay u double what u would get paid to make up for it.*
Sunny: *I couldn't do that!*
Gabe: *I want to spend time with u. And I won't take no for an answer, but I don't want u to suffer financially because of it. So do what u can.*
Sunny: *Ok. Well, I have to go get ready for work.*
Gabe: *Ok. Have a good day. I'll call u later to figure out when we can meet during the week. Don't think I'm waiting 'til the weekend to see u.*
Sunny: *LOL! Fine. Enjoy your day.*
Gabe: *Later, Sweet Girl.*

~~~

Later at work, Sunny was on cloud nine. She had switched on and off between working and trying to find anyone who would change shifts with her, so she could have the weekend off. She knew that Gabe was willing her pay her, but she just didn't feel right taking his money like that. And she definitely hated leaving her co-workers hanging, on the busy weekend. She may have hated retail, but that didn't mean others had to suffer for it. So she had even hunted down some co-workers' numbers and called to beg them. And finally someone had come through for her, a super sweet new girl named Vanessa. Sunny thought that she'd have to find a way to repay her at some point. Weekends were sacred in the retail world, because you never had them off.

"Okay. Spill it!" One of her work friends, Becca broke into her woolgathering.

"Huh? Spill what?" Sunny tried to dodge.

"I know you're a happy person, but this is ridiculous. There's being happy and jokingly grumbling about the rude customers. And then there's being so happy that when a customer calls you a 'stupid bitch', you just respond with a 'have a nice day' and actually mean it!" Becca looked at her incredulously.

"She called me a 'stupid bitch'?!" Sunny stared after the retreating customer.

"YES! That's exactly what I mean. You didn't even notice! So, spill it. What has you so oblivious to everything around you? And can I get some of it?!"

"Oh, it's nothing. I just met someone really nice. And I was able to get that new girl Vanessa to switch with me, so I could have the weekend off to spend with him." Sunny explained, remaining vague about the details.

"Oh my God! You finally met someone?! That is huge news! Did you finally get some, because you have that glow about you, and I know it's been a minute since you've had a hot beef injection?" Becca made the 'duck face' and gestured crudely with her hips.

"You are truly sick!" Sunny struggled to hold back her laughter when a customer spotted Becca's sexually suggestive movements and scuttled away in disgust.

"Ha. You know it's true. So did you get some?" Becca prodded further.

Sunny could see she wasn't going to let this go. "No, I didn't. But let's just say he's a great kisser, so the bedroom action looks promising."

"Ain't that the truth?! I've never met a bad kisser that was good in bed." Becca turned up her nose.

"Amen, honey!" Their gay co-worker and friend Santiago piped in, walking up in the middle of their conversation. "And the same is true for a bad dancer. If you can't work those hips on the dance floor, then what can you do for me in the sack?!" Santiago and Becca laughed, high-fiving each other.

Sunny realized this conversation had gone straight down the

gutter quickly. "Uh, guys? We should really get back to work, before we get our asses reamed."

"Fine. But I better get details when you come back from your weekend with him. Because I hope you know that you're getting down with him." At Sunny's perplexed look Becca explained further. "Spending the weekend means staying over-night. A stay over-night means getting busy. God, Sunny you are so innocent sometimes, I think you're still a virgin!"

"You're a nut." Sunny shook her head and went to go fold the clothes that a customer destroyed earlier.

Oh God! Is he really gonna want to have sex with me this weekend? But she guessed that after their first date he kind of deserved it. *Poor guy.*

And Sunny really wanted to…never wanted something so badly her whole life. Her body's reaction to him was indescribable. So she couldn't imagine how it would react once they finally had actual sex. But that meant baring all and getting naked in front of him. She had trouble getting naked in front of regular guys. Guys with hair in weird places and potbellies. So getting naked in front of a man the whole world viewed as perfection, was a bit intimidating. Even if the more time she spent with him, she saw him more as Gabriel Wolf the man, not the actor. But it was still there nagging at her. *The only thing I can do is just go with it, stop worrying and enjoy the weekend.*

~~~

The next morning Sunny woke up to the now customary text from Gabe.

Gabe: *Good morning, Sweet Girl.*

She loved when he called her that. She melted into a puddle of butter every time. And she was excited that they were developing sweet routines. Almost every night so far he would call her, even if it was briefly, to wish her a goodnight. And every morning he would text her.

Sunny: *Good morning, Mr. Wolf.*

Gabe: *How r u? Did you sleep well?*
Sunny: *I slept great. I put on one of ur movies to fall asleep to.*
Gabe: *I hope that means that u wanted to fall asleep to my face and not because it's boring. Which movie?*
Sunny: *Of course the former. None of ur movies are boring. The one where ur kicking ass & taking names. :)*
Gabe: *Isn't that all my movies? LOL! ;)*
Sunny: *No, not all. But this one u take ur shirt off a lot. :P*
Gabe: *Uh, huh. That's not fair that you've seen me with no shirt, but I haven't seen u without one.*

Oh, God! Sunny buried her face in her hands. *Don't wanna think about it!*

Sunny: *Maybe someday... Well I better get moving. Have to start getting ready for work and call my mom for our weekly Sunday phone call.*
Gabe: *I know ur avoiding the subject. And that's ok, but I'm getting that beautiful curvy body naked sooner or later. Enjoy talking with ur mom. Tell her about me. Lunch, tomorrow?*

Damn! That man has the intuition of an over-protective mother! Was she really that easy to read? Well the answer was staring her in the face in the form of a text. So she guessed, yes, yes she was.

Sunny: *Ok, I have to be at work by 2. So how about noon?*
Gabe: *Perfect. I'll come get u.*
Sunny: *Ok. See u tomorrow.*
Gabe: *Later, Sweet Girl.*
Sunny looked at the time on her phone. She only had about an hour before she had to start getting ready for work, so she knew she had to call her mom now. She brought up her mom's number and hit call.
"Hey, Sweetie Pie!" Her mom answered.

"Hi, mom. How are you? How's dad?"

"We're good, baby. What's going on with you? You sound awfully happy this morning." Sunny could hear the smile through the phone.

Well, here we go. Let's get right to the point. "Well mom, I've met someone." Sunny cringed as her mother whooped into the phone.

"I knew it! I've been waiting for you to say that for a long time now." Sunny could hear her mom turning away from the phone to talk to her dad. "Sam honey, your daughter has met herself a man!"

"MOM! You don't have to tell dad just yet." Sunny shook her head in embarrassment.

"What? I can't be happy for my little girl?"

"Sure you can, but it's still new. And I want to be sure before I shout it from the rooftops."

"Well, I guess you're right. I just got excited, is all. So tell me about him." Donna asked curiously.

Sunny knew she had a choice. Either fess up now and tell her mother who she was really dating or wait until it came out in some crappy tabloid. And she knew eventually it would end up in a filthy rag magazine. She just wanted to stay in fairytale land a little bit longer, before facing reality. But when it came to her mom, she had to make a choice now.

"Well mom…he's kind of an actor." Sunny braced herself.

"Oh, Sunny! You have to find a man with a more stable job than that. Does he even work regularly?" Sunny's mom scolded her.

You have no idea, mom! "Yes mom, he does get regular work."

"Well then, do I know him? Have I seen him in anything? What's his name?" Her mother asked skeptically.

"Uh, yeah. Well, you see, I'm kinda seeing Gabriel Wolf." Sunny cringed for the second time. Her mother may not be a movie connoisseur like she was, but her mother knew a few super-hot actors, and Gabe was one of them.

"WHAT?! You mean that boy who they named 'Sexiest Man in the World'? You're dating him?!" Her mother screeched into the phone.

"Yes, mother. Is that so hard to believe?" Sunny rolled her eyes, only because her mother couldn't see it.

"No, of course not! I know how beautiful you are, but most famous people stick together. It's rare you hear of them dating or marrying someone that's not in the spotlight too. That can be a hard road, sweetie. Are you sure you can deal with all that comes with his fame and fortune?" Sunny could hear the concern in her mom's voice.

"I don't know mom. But I do know that I love h-", Sunny clapped a hand over her mouth. *Love! Only after a few days?* She knew it seemed impossible, but didn't make it any less true.

"Oh honey, please just don't get hurt. Don't get me wrong, I know when love comes it can happen in the blink of an eye. But this isn't love with just anyone. Just be careful. That's all I have to say." She could tell Donna had a lot more to say than that, but she was trying to restrain herself.

"Thanks mom. I love you, you know?"

"Yeah, I know. So tell me is he a good kisser?" Well, the hard part of the conversation was over. Now her mother had moved to the fun part.

Sunny finished up her call with her mother, promising to call her sooner than next Sunday if she needed her or had any juicy stories to tell. They were close, but not *that* close. She drew the line at the details of her sex life. So with that, she put her phone down on the coffee table and headed to her tiny bathroom to get ready for work.

~~~

Monday at noon, Gabe was waiting outside of Sunny's apartment building. He was thinking that he couldn't wait for the day when she finally invited him in. Someone's personal space said so much about them. Hell, he couldn't wait to show her his home in Malibu, but she wasn't ready for that yet. But he had every hope that by the end of this weekend, that would be different. If he couldn't have her, taste her, bury himself inside her, he was going to lose his mind.

Sunny stepped outside in a pair of black dress slacks, a bright fuchsia top, a short-sleeved gray jacket and wide black belt that had a big faux leather bow on it. She looked like a gift he very much wanted to unwrap.

"You look adorable." He greeted her with a bear hug that lifted her off her feet, and a kiss.

She giggled delightfully. "You don't look so bad yourself, handsome."

"Are these your work clothes", he asked straightening the lapels of her jacket when he put her down.

"Yeah, I figured I'd just head straight to work from lunch. So where are we headed?" She asked while he opened the truck door for her to get in.

"Well, since I know how much you love movies, how would you feel about eating lunch from a real-life gourmet movie set food truck?"

"Seriously?!" Sunny shouted and bounced up and down like a kid in a candy store.

Seeing her reaction was well worth eating food he'd had a million times before. "Seriously."

"Sweet!" She wrapped her arms around his shoulders and gave him a big squeeze and peck on the cheek.

Gabe opened the passenger door for her, walked to the driver's side, slid in and put the truck in drive and headed back to the set, which luckily wasn't far from her apartment. Once they were there, he parked the truck, came around to open the door for her and entwined her fingers with his as he led her onto the set.

Today they were filming at a fancy historical bank. But since it was lunchtime, the cast and crew were milling about eating, talking or resting in various places. Sunny looked around with her mouth opened in awe. She was just too cute.

He walked her over to a group of men, to introduce her.

"Hey guys, this is Madison Stone, though she goes by Sunny."
They all said some form of 'hello'. "Sunny, this is Kyle Higgins,
the director. Greg Jensen the assistant director. And Thomas
Keats the cinematographer."

Sunny reached out to shake hands with each man as he
introduced them. "Hello gentlemen, it's so nice to meet you. Mr.
Higgins, I saw your movie Burned that won best documentary at
the *Sundance Film Festival*. It was phenomenal! I bawled like a
baby through most of it." She smiled brightly.

"Thank you, Sunny. Call me Kyle."

And just like that, she had turned on her classic 'Sunny-
charm' and the men were instantly enamored. How she did it,
Gabe couldn't fathom.

They talked to the men for a few more moments then Gabe
directed Sunny to the food truck. They picked their items and
then headed over to one of the picnic tables that had been set out
for everyone.

"We could also eat our lunch in my trailer, if you'd like?"
Gabe suggested slyly.

"If I know you that would be a bad idea. As much as I'd like
some alone time with you, I don't think we'd actually get around
to eating. And I'd hate for my first time on a real-life movie set to
be wasted inside a trailer. Plus, if the trailer got to rockin' that
would make for a pretty bad first impression, don't you think?"
Sunny scolded him.

"Dammit! Why do you have to be so sensible?!" Gabe
grumbled, good-naturedly.

Sunny just giggled and started eating. Gabe loved that she
wasn't some 'salad-eating' girl. She liked food and wasn't afraid
to show it, a Midwest steak and potatoes kind of girl, all the way.
In fact, involving most things, she seemed pretty comfortable in
her own skin; dancing around, singing in front of a crowd and
being silly. It was her sensuality that she had trouble with. In the
moment she blossomed, but before and after she doubted herself.
She needed to put that doubt to rest, because as far as he was
concerned her body was made for sex. Like *Jessica Rabbit*, but

shorter.

"What?" Sunny looked at him warily.

Gabe hadn't realized that he was staring at her. He decided that it would only help to tell her exactly why he was staring.

"I was just thinking that you have a body that's made for sex, like a more compact version of *Jessica Rabbit*. It's ridiculous that you doubt yourself so much." He whispered in her ear, so no one else could hear.

She swallowed loudly, "Uh…ahhh…I literally have no response to that." She stared down at her food as if it was the most interesting thing she'd ever seen. A telltale flush spreading across her plump cheeks.

"You don't have to say anything, just take it in and start believing it." He leaned in and kissed her softly on the cheek.

"Alright." She still sounded doubtful.

This weekend, he was *so* going to enjoy convincing her. His pants were getting tight just thinking about all that he wanted to do to her.

"So are you going to tell me what we're doing this weekend? Or will it be another surprise?"

"Another surprise."

"Okay, dress code?"

"All I can tell you is to pack a light overnight bag. The days should be fairly warm and the nights cool, so bring clothes according to that. Pajamas optional." He winked at her.

"I'll keep that in mind."

~~~

After they finished eating, they had about forty-five minutes before Sunny needed Gabe to drop her back off at her car to head to work. So he spent some time showing her around and introducing her to the cast.

She got to meet the child actors that played his kids in the movie, who were super sweet and could hold conversation like adults. Then she met Jessica Hall, the actress that played his wife.

Sunny couldn't put her finger on it, but the woman just seemed a little too full of herself. And last, Gabe introduced her to the guys that played the bank robbers. They seemed like anything but 'bad guys', well personality-wise. They had the rough look to them for the role, but seemed really nice. The actor that played the leader of the bank robbers was someone that Sunny recognized from several previous movies, Josiah Caldwell. He seemed well on his way to *Gabriel Wolf* status.

But where Gabe was dark, he was all light. He had blond hair, green eyes and long lankiness. He wasn't as tall as Gabe, but close. He definitely wasn't as massive as Gabe. And there was the fact that he was a big flirt. Sunny chuckled to herself, as Gabe quickly extricated her from the situation, claiming that he wanted to show her his movie trailer.

"Welcome to my home away from home." Gabe swept his arm the length of the big trailer.

"This is way bigger than I thought it would be." Sunny looked around in shock.

"Trust me. I've had my fair share of tiny digs in the past. And I'm a big guy, so I would spend as little time in those as I could."

"Yeah I bet. You're kinda making even this one feel crowded." Sunny craned her neck to look around him.

"Oh am I crowding you?" Gabe stepped closer, making her take a step back, which she found wasn't far.

The back of her knees hit the bed. She lost her balance and her butt plopped down on the mattress.

"Hmm…now I've got you, right where I want you. In bed." Gabe started to crawl over her, making her fall all the way back onto the bed.

He covered her with his upper body and settled his lower half between her legs. Their bodies lined up perfectly for her to feel his perpetual hardness against her arousal. Her hips begged her to move, wanting that friction that she craved. But knowing they couldn't finish, she remained still, not wanting to get him worked up again.

Luckily he somewhat distracted her, by cupping her face with both hands and looking at her intently. He caressed her face from temple to chin and then across her cheeks. The whole time just studying her, his vivid blue eyes blazing a trail over her every feature. She felt so naked. Never had she felt anything as intense as the connection she had with him.

"Sunny...I-", Gabe started in a voice thick with emotion, but then a quick knock and the door opening, completely killed the moment.

"Hey Gabe, it's...oh, nice! Hey, we could make it a threesome", Josiah interrupted, coming into the trailer. Gabe didn't move, continuing to cover Sunny as if shielding her nakedness. And she did feel utterly exposed. Gabe had stripped her bare in that moment, and Josiah coming in a second later, had her feeling severely vulnerable.

Oh, this guy wasn't just a flirt he was a bit of an inconsiderate douche too, Sunny thought reevaluating her first impression of him. Gabe's voice went from gentle warmth to cold steel, "I'd watch your fucking mouth, if I were you Josiah."

"Aw man! I was just messing around. I just came to tell you that cameras roll in fifteen." Josiah raised his hands up defensively.

"Thanks. Now get out." Gabe's voice was deceptively soft. Like the louder someone was the more they're trying to overcompensate for false bravado, but the deadly calm and quiet voice said 'ass-whooping' for anyone who crosses me. And Josiah recognized it for what it was, and slowly backed out of the trailer like he was afraid to turn his back on Gabe. Sunny hoped that he never used that voice on her. *Yikes!*

"I'm so sorry Sunny." Gabe finally lifted his weight and warmth off of her. Leaving her feeling chilled.

"Don't apologize for that asshole." Sunny grumbled, still needing to know what Gabe had been about to say.

"Well I better hurry up and get you back to your car, so you can get to work." He held out his hand to her, to pull her up from the bed.

"Thank you for bringing me here. It was so exciting and lunch was great!" Sunny stood on her tiptoes and kissed him softly on the lips.

"No problem. I liked having you here." He smiled down at her. "Now scoot and skedaddle, little lady!" He said in his best cowboy impersonation, playfully swatting her on the butt, making her jump and run to the door, giggling.

~~~

When Gabe got back to the set from dropping Sunny off, he walked straight towards Josiah. Josiah saw him coming and again raised his hands defensively.

"Hey man, no harm no foul! I'd probably be pissed off too if someone came barging into my trailer when I had a hot plump little chocolate number like that under me." Josiah laughed.

The laugh quickly died, when Gabe grabbed him by the scruff of his collar and nearly lifted him off of his feet. Gabe wanted to smash his face in so badly, but knew that Kyle and the producers would have his ass if he messed up Josiah's face.

"I don't ever want to see you fucking near her again. Don't talk to her, don't even fucking look at her. Do you hear me, you little shit?!" Gabe felt hands wrap around his arms and shoulders, and vaguely registered calming voices in his ear. Finally he let Josiah go.

"Fuck dude! You're gonna act like a pussy-whipped little bitch over *that* girl?!" Josiah straightened his shirt indignantly.

It took nearly every male crew member they had to stop Gabe from killing him, as he lunged at Josiah.

"Josiah, go back to your trailer. Gabe, go walk it off. Now!" Kyle yelled at them both.

Gabe stormed off, not even sure of what direction he was headed in. He walked a few blocks, and then started back. Once he was back on set, he went straight to his trailer, not quite ready to see Josiah yet.

He sat on the couch and put his head in his hands. He hadn't been that violently angry since he was a kid. Then, it had been over his hurt from being abandoned and unwanted. Now, it was because he was fiercely protective over the only person he had ever let into his heart, the only person who seemed to want *him*...the real him.

Josiah was harmless. He had just gotten under his skin. But what would happen when someone did want to cause her harm? He would lose his shit!

A knock sounded on the door. "Gabe? It's Kyle."

"Come in." Gabe sighed.

"Hey Gabe, you alright?" Kyle looked at him with concern.

"Yeah, I'm good. Sorry man, I didn't mean to lose my shit like that."

"It's okay. I heard what Josiah said, he was being dick. And to be honest, it's nice to see you so happy. I've known you for a while. And I've never seen you act like that with a woman, or anyone for that matter. I'm glad she found you." Kyle smiled.

"Yeah, she's amazing. The best person I've ever met." His heart warmed thinking about Sunny's smile.

Kyle stood up and patted Gabe on the arm. "Then I'd say you'd better keep her close. Don't be an idiot and let her go. Hell, I'll kick your ass if you do. I think she's been the reason for your great performances lately. I can't risk losing that." He winked at him. "Plus, she seems like a sweet girl. Everyone on the set loved her." He walked to the door, "Take a few more minutes and then get your ass out there and take your anger out on Josiah in your scene with him. I need that shit on camera." He chuckled as he let himself out of the trailer.

Gabe quietly thought about what Kyle had said. He knew it was good advice, all of it. So with that; Gabe stood up, took a deep breath, cracked his neck, and then headed out the door.

~~~

The rest of the week passed slowly for Sunny. Waiting for the much anticipated weekend, was like watching paint dry. And what made it worse was the fact that she was busy, working every day up until Saturday and Gabe's schedule was even more hectic. They were filming sixteen hour days and Gabe had no time to get away. So they were relegated to phone and text conversations. But there was one thing that could keep Sunny busy for at least one evening…shopping.

She wasn't a huge fan of shopping, especially when money was always tight. But she had yet to spend any of the bonus she'd received last month from work. And now she actually had something to shop for. A weekend full of Gabriel Wolf seemed like as good a reason as any to shop. The main items on the itinerary were: a fun flirty dress for Saturday night and she needed something jaw-dropping for underneath.

It was Thursday evening, so that only left her a day and a half to find something. So Sunny of course recruited the help of Alyssa, who naturally ended up with more bags than Sunny did. Sunny had already gotten everything that she needed. She had found the perfect cocktail dress that her pink wedge heels would match with perfectly. And she found a sexy bra and panty set with pink details the same color as the pink in the dress and her shoes.

Sunny knew that this weekend was going to change everything in their relationship. Sex was a huge step, but also an inevitable one…a foregone conclusion. So she had to be ready for it. She wasn't going to get caught in some crazy flower print Granny Panties.

As they walked through the mall Sunny spotted *Barnes & Noble* her favorite bookstore. She could get lost in there for hours. And the wall o' journals tempted her every time.

"Hey Alyssa, I want to go into the *Barnes & Noble* really quick."

"Don't you have their e-reader? Why would you need to go in?"

"Yes, but there's nothing like the smell of books and I just feel smarter being in there." Sunny stuck out her tongue at her friend.

"Fine. I wanted to check out some of the magazines anyway."

They went in separate directions, Sunny towards the romance section and Alyssa to the newsstand. She went to the romance section out of habit, but for the first time she felt uninterested. Maybe it was because for the first time in a long time she actually had a romance of her own.

Sunny had only walked away from Alyssa a minute ago, but she heard footsteps running and Alyssa calling her name.

"I'm over here, Alyssa. What's wrong?" Sunny tried not to yell too loudly in the quiet store.

Alyssa flew around the corner with a couple of magazines clutched in her hands. "Sunny, you've got to see this!"

Sunny's little insulated bubble of happiness popped the minute she looked at the covers of each magazine. Her stomach dropped as she saw several grainy pictures of herself and Gabe in different degrees of intimacy; hugging, kissing and holding hands on their first date. One magazine topped the rest with three crystal clear pictures of them on Monday on the set of his current movie. The first picture was when they were sitting at the picnic table and he was comparing her to *Jessica Rabbit*. The second was him kissing her cheek. And the third was of them coming out of his trailer.

The multiple headlines read: *GABRIEL WOLF'S NEW MAIN SQUEEZE! WHO'S GABRIEL'S NEW LUCKY LADY? DOES GABRIEL WOLF HAVE A NEW LADY?* And the one to top them all: *GABRIEL ADMITS- 'I LIKE BIG BUTTS AND I CANNOT LIE!'*

The last one finally brought the tears to her eyes that had been clogged in her throat since Alyssa first showed her the crap tabloids. *Ha! Really fucking funny!* Her hands started to shake uncontrollably and the magazines tumbled to the floor.

"Aw, Sunny don't cry!" Alyssa sat her in a wooden chair and dug through her purse for a tissue.

"I…kn…knew it…wa…was coming." Sunny choked out. "I just…wa…wanted…it to la…last longer."

"Just calm down sweetie. I'm gonna go to the *Starbuck's* and get you something to drink. Maybe you should call Gabe. He knows how to handle this stuff." Alyssa soothed.

"I can't talk to him li...like...this!" Sunny wailed.

"Here, give me your phone. I'll call him for you." Alyssa grabbed her phone and walked off to the coffee shop. Sunny was too distraught to care.

A few moments later Alyssa came back with a bottle of water and a cookie to cheer Sunny up and some tissue to wipe her face. Sunny took the water and tissue gratefully, but ignored the cookie. If she ate anything right now she would totally barf.

"Okay, I'm gonna take you home now." Alyssa looked at her with concern as Sunny sobbed quietly.

They walked out of the building, a few people looking on curiously. *If they only knew.*

~~~

They were wrapping up filming for the day and Gabe had just walked into his trailer to check if he had any messages from Sunny when his phone started ringing, her name appearing on the screen.

"Hey, Sweet Girl." Gabe smiled into the phone.

"Gabe, its Alyssa!" Hearing her friend's voice instead of Sunny's instantly sent him into a panic.

"What's wrong?!"

"Well we're at the bookstore and I saw all these tabloids with you and Sunny's pictures on them. She saw them, freaked out and is now bawling her eyes out." Alyssa blurted it all into the phone quickly.

"Fuck! I knew this was gonna happen.
Fuck...fuck...FUCK!" He pulled his phone away and screamed in his trailer.

"I didn't know what to do, so I called you. I figured you'd know how to handle this kind of stuff. But I don't think she's able to talk on the phone at the moment."

"Get her home now, I'll meet you there." Gabe hung up the phone before she could respond, grabbed his jacket and keys and ran out the door.

He knew that he was probably closer to her apartment than she was. So there was no need for him to rush like a maniac, but he did anyway. He had to be there when she got home.

He parked on the street, got out of his truck and started pacing in front of her building. He was sure that people would think he was a stalker if they saw him pacing, but he couldn't help it. He also didn't doubt that there was some douchebag paparazzi lying in wait to get the perfect photo op, and he only made it worse hanging around outside her building. But he needed to know that she was okay and make sure that she knew this didn't change anything between them.

A little silver car pulled up then and Sunny and Alyssa got out of the car. His gut squeezed at Sunny's dejected face. Her eyes were swollen and red and her cheeks still wet from recently shed tears. And the moment she saw him standing there, her bottom lip started to tremble and the dam broke again. His heart broke at her tears and not being able to stand it anymore he ran to her and scooped her up into his arms. She wrapped her arms around his neck in a death grip and sobbed into his shoulder.

"Can you get the door for me?" He asked looking back at Alyssa.

"Yeah, sure." Alyssa walked ahead of them to punch in the door code and open the door.

Gabe walked in, but had no idea which way to go. "Baby, I need you to tell me where to go."

"This fl…floor, apartment one-oh-four." She pointed in the direction he needed to go and he walked down the hall.

"Okay, Sweet Girl, we're here. I'm gonna put you down to get your keys." Gabe said after he stopped in front of her door.

Once he put her down, she searched through her purse herself for her keys. But once she got them out, her hands shook too hard to get it in the lock. He gently took them from her and opened the door. She walked in and switched on the light, as he followed her.

Her apartment was a tiny studio. It was minimal, but with small feminine touches here and there to make the space her own. There were flower stencils on the walls, candles in random spots and a string of little white lights that had little paper lanterns on each one.

Sunny sat on a futon that must have doubled as her bed, since he didn't see an actual bed anywhere. She had so little, but asked for nothing. He'd give her the world if she'd let him.

"Sunny-"

"I'm sorry, Gabe." Sunny interrupted him. "I know I'm overreacting to all of this. It just took me by surprise."

He came over to sit next to her and pulled her into his arms. "Sweetie, it's okay. This isn't something that you're used to."

"But I knew! I knew it was coming. Anyone you date is going to make headlines. I just didn't expect to feel so…so violated." She pulled away from him and started to wring her hands together.

"I know, baby. It will just take some getting used to."

"I don't know, Gabe. There were like four or five of those magazines. And most were harmless, but one was just mean. And it's only going to get worse. I just don't think I can do this." Her voice broke at the end of the sentence.

No no no no no! He grabbed Sunny's shoulders and forced her to turn and look at him. "Sunny please don't do this! You've come to mean so much to me in such a short amount of time. I can't imagine you not in my life. Just come away with me for the weekend. And if you feel the same after, I'll let you go." He knew that was a lie but he had to convince her to spend more time with him.

She didn't say anything for a while.

"Please, Sunny." Gabe begged one more time.

"Okay." She said so softly he barely heard her.

"Thank you." He pulled her to him, raining kisses all over her face until she actually started giggling.

The sound was like music to his ears.

~~~

Gabe had stayed a little while longer last night, making sure that she was truly okay. And then with a tender goodbye kiss, he left to let her get some sleep. She had called Alyssa to let her know that she was doing okay. Alyssa had her bags of new clothes for the weekend and would hold them for her until she got off work tonight. Sunny was glad that she only had one more day to get through.

As Sunny drove into work, she thought about how much her life was probably about to change. There was no doubt in her mind that she had fallen in love with Gabe. Especially after the thought of ending it with him practically brought her to her knees. And she wanted, needed him in her life. But the question was, would she be strong enough to handle the scrutiny? Maybe she could just avoid the magazines in the checkout lines at the grocery store, the articles online and shows like *TMZ* and *Extra*. Little did she know, avoiding speculation was going to be harder than she realized.

She walked into work and noticed that several of her co-workers were staring at her. Once she got to the break room, she realized why people were staring. On the tables were a few of the tabloids that she had seen last night. She quickly grabbed them and shoved them onto one of the shelves out of sight. Just then, Becca and Santiago came barreling into the room and surrounded her.

"Oh my God! You're dating Gabriel Wolf?!" Santiago screamed.

"I can't believe you didn't tell me!" Becca shrieked.

"I didn't say anything because of this very reason." Sunny pointed at both of them. "I didn't want to be bombarded with a billion questions and looked at differently. Plus, I had no idea if it was even gonna go anywhere."

"Well you can't date a mega-star and not expect us to ask you questions!" Becca whined.

"And by those pics, I'd definitely say things are just heating up." Santiago said in a bitchy tone.

It was like they hadn't even heard her. "I need to clock in and get to work guys. I'll talk to you later."

"You better."

"We need more details. Stop holding out on us!"

Sunny didn't care who said what, she just kept walking. They were her friends, but not like Alyssa. They had big mouths and even bigger judgmental attitudes, with a higher probability of talking smack behind any and everyone's back. *Tomorrow can't come quick enough.*

Chapter 9

Finally Saturday had come and Sunny woke up feeling like it was Christmas morning. The rest of her day at work had been sheer torture; dodging her friends, finding work to keep busy in order to avoid everyone's questions and just in general, being anxious about the coming weekend. Now that it was finally here, she was so excited she danced a little jig into her bathroom to start getting ready.

The only thing that slightly tainted her feeling of joy was the plan that they had to devise last night in order to avoid the paparazzi and their intrusive cameras. Sunny and Gabe had come up with the plan and she had relayed it to Alyssa, who would help them pull it off.

After taking her shower, where she had meticulously shaved every part of her body, she then buffed and lotioned her skin within an inch of its life. Now she was as soft and smooth as a baby's bottom. Her hair freshly washed, she threw in some product and blow-dried her hair into a soft mass of wild corkscrew curls that fell around her shoulders. She bypassed makeup and just opted for some *Burt's Bees* lip balm instead. She figured she'd get all dolled up later. Then she packed her overnight bag, checking it nervously three times before she was satisfied that she wasn't forgetting anything. Then her phone rang with Alyssa's assigned ringtone.

"Hey!" Sunny answered.

"Hello Super-Secret Agent Stone. Are you ready to begin your mission?" Alyssa said in some ridiculous imitation of a masculine voice.

"Ha! Yeah I know all of this is stupid. But to avoid the paparazzi following us, pictures and more stories, we have to do this. But thank you for helping me." Sunny said in barely concealed frustration.

"You're welcome. You know I'd do anything for you girl." Alyssa assured her.

"I know. So I'll meet you in the parking garage in five minutes." Sunny said switching into her own super-secret agent voice.

"Okay. See you in a few." Alyssa said before hanging up.

Sunny was meeting Gabe at the boat docks at ten a.m., which was in ten minutes. She was giddy with anticipation as she walked out the backdoor of her building, with her overnight bag and purse. She met Alyssa in the parking garage, got into the back seat of Alyssa's car and laid down out of sight. They knew as long as no one spotted her leaving the garage, they'd have no idea where she ended up.

The drive to the docks only took a few minutes, her and Alyssa cracking jokes and giggling over the absurdity of what she had to do to spend time with a guy. But he wasn't just any man. The acting part aside, he was the sweetest, sexiest and most considerate man she'd ever known. The car pulled to a stop and Sunny peeked to look around.

"Are you sure no one was following you?" Sunny asked Alyssa.

"I'm positive."

With the coast clear, Sunny sat up and saw Gabe walking towards them. It was a cool morning, so he had on worn jeans and a cream fisherman's cable knit sweater, that made his shoulders look even more enormous. And he was sporting his sexy as hell gray newsboy hat pulled low over his eyes, just like he had the night they'd met.

Once he got to the car, he walked around to Sunny's door, opened it and helped her out, kissed her on the lips and then grabbed her bag to carry for her.

"Oh, you two make me sick! Have a great weekend!"

Alyssa's voice switched from mock disgust to jovial, making them laugh.

"Thanks Alyssa, for bringing her." Gabe said sincerely.

"No prob." Alyssa waved as she pulled off.

Now alone again for the first time since his trailer on Monday, Sunny felt the sexual tension pouring off of them. Her skin instantly flushed and she wondered if she really needed her sweatshirt because it was getting a little warm already.

Gabe squeezed her hand. "Are you ready, Sweet Girl?"

"Aye-aye, Cap'n!" She said with a cheeky grin.

He walked her over to a beautiful sleek medium sized boat. She knew almost nothing about boats, but she knew they came bigger or smaller than this one. That was Gabe, never trying to get the best of the best. He wanted just enough to satisfy his needs and nothing more.

And luckily it wasn't a sailboat because she knew that she wouldn't be much help in that department. It was more like a modest yacht.

"So are you renting this for the weekend or is she yours?" Sunny asked looking up at him.

"She's mine. I drove her down from Malibu."

"Well, she's a beautiful boat. But you named her 'Sea Wench'?!" Sunny looked at the name painted on the back and laughed.

"Actually, I've already decided to change it when we get back."

"Really? To what?"

"Sweet Girl."

Sunny's mouth gaped for a moment, then she firmly shut it before she swallowed a bug.

"You're naming her after me? Isn't naming your boat after someone a big commitment, *Forrest Gump*?" Sunny squeezed her lips together to keep from laughing.

"I'm ready if you are, *Jenny*." Again her mouth just flopped around with no sound coming out. So he just laughed and pulled her towards the boat. "Let's get going Gilligan, times a-wasting."

With the agility and grace of a lion, Gabe jumped onto the boat. Then as Sunny climbed up, he raised his hands, gripped her under her arms and lowered her to the deck. If they were together a million years, she'd never get tired of him picking her up like she weighed nothing. No guys *ever* tried to pick her up.

After showing her around his boat, Gabe pulled her over to the captain's chair. He started the engine and pulled her between his legs as he sat down. He put her hands on the steering wheel and covered them with his, as he helped her guide the boat out of the dock into open water.

"This is so cool! I love boats! I don't know anything about them, but I love 'em." Sunny couldn't hide the excitement in her voice.

"Good. I was praying you weren't the kind of person that gets seasick." Gabe said before kissing her neck softly.

"Nope. I love the water. So can I finally know where we're headed?" She craned her head back to look at him.

He tipped his chin forward, making her look at the island ahead.

"Ah, Catalina?! Sweet, I haven't gotten a chance to go there yet! You make good choices." She smiled back at him radiantly.

"Well, I figured it was close enough that we didn't have to spend half of our weekend traveling, but far enough to feel like a different world." He leaned down and kissed the sensitive skin right below her ear.

"It's perfect." She shuttered.

"Would you like to go straight into Avalon Bay or would you like to sail around the whole island first?"

"I'd like to sail around first."

"Alright. If you'd like you can sit on the couch and take in the sights." Gabe offered.

"Nope. I like it just fine where I'm at." She snuggled her back closer into his wide chest.

"Good." He wrapped his arms around her waist, pulling her closer still.

As they made their way around the island, Gabe watched as Sunny looked around in awe. He loved the way she held such joy in the things that many people took for granted on a daily basis, including him. Being with her made him see and feel things, as if it was the first time. He wondered if that was the way he'd feel when they finally made love.

Enjoying the sail around the island, Sunny seemed relaxed enough for Gabe to broach a subject she had been avoiding.

"So I was wondering, did you go to college?" Gabe tried to ease into the conversation.

"Yes, *Columbia College* in Chicago." Sunny answered right away, not knowing exactly where he was going with the question.

"What did you major in?"

"Creative Writing." She answered hesitantly, finally understanding.

"So you are a writer. I remember Alyssa mentioning it the first night we met."

"Yes and no, I guess." Sunny hedged.

"Why do you say that? Do you write?"

"Yes."

"Well then, you're a writer."

"I write, but none of it has been recognized. Then again I haven't really put my stuff out there either." Sunny tried shrugging it off. But Gabe wasn't giving up that easily.

"And why not?"

"I don't know. Fear I guess."

"What do you write exactly? Novels?"

"No. It doesn't really matter." Sunny tried to dodge.

"Come on, tell me." Gabe pried.

"I really don't think it's a good idea." Sunny tried to step away from him.

He quickly grabbed her and held her against him. "I'm not letting go until you tell me. I don't see what the big deal is."

"I write screenplays, okay?!" She blurted out quickly.

"Really?! Why wouldn't you want to tell me that?" Gabe asked perplexed.

"Because I didn't want you to think that was the reason why I'm interested in you." She snapped in frustration.

"Oh Sweet Girl, trust me if that was the only reason you were interested, you would've mentioned it within the first couple of hours of knowing me. Trust me, I know. I've been dealing with that for years."

"Plus, I guess I was worried that you would want to see my work and then not like it." She said this softly and self-consciously.

"Aw baby! I doubt anything you've created would be bad. And don't you understand that I've been reading screenplays for several years, so I know what's good or not? So if your stuff needed some work, I'd be the exact person to help you perfect it?" Gabe reasoned.

"Hmm…I never really thought of it that way." Sunny frowned, deep in thought.

"Exactly! I bet we'd make a great team. When we get back Sunday evening, I want you to give me all your work. I'll read it and then we can go over what needs work. And what doesn't need work, I'll see if I can get it into the right hands as soon as possible." Gabe felt the excitement build up inside of him at the thought of being able to help her realize her dream.

"You'd really do that for me?" Sunny turned to look in his eyes, her honey-brown eyes melting his heart.

"Haven't you realized yet, that I'd do anything for you?" Her eyes got all glassy with unshed tears. And she turned in his arms, slipped her hands around his neck and buried her face in the crook between his neck and shoulder. He gripped the steering wheel with one hand and held her close with the other.

"Thank you." Her words were muffled against his neck.

They made it back around the island an hour later. Gabe steered the boat into a spot at the dock. He jumped down and tied the boat off, then came back to help Sunny down. He couldn't wait for her to see the beach house that he had rented for the weekend.

"Do you mind walking? We're not staying far from here." Gabe asked.

"No, it's a beautiful day, walking would be perfect."

Sunny took the hand he held out to her and they walked hand in hand towards the beach house. As they walked they watched different boats coming and going. Sunny pointed out to him a boat that looked like a pirate ship that she had seen a couple times docked at *Shoreline Village*. They picked out houses built in the hills that they wouldn't mind living in, noticing that they had similar tastes.

Making it to the house, Gabe was happy with what he chose. It was right off the beach and private. Half on stilts and half supported by the hills. It had bright blue siding with white trim and the stairs leading up to it were also painted white. He led Sunny up the stairs and into the spacious entryway and living room. Everything was decorated with an elegant beachy feel to it. It was very bright and airy with different tones of blue, tan and white.

"Come on, let's check out the rest." He started to pull her towards the rest of the house.

They looked in at the large open kitchen that overlooked the living room. Then they walked down the hall and Gabe switched on the light in the bathroom. It had a big shower with glass doors and an enormous tub for two, with double sinks. It had two entrances, one from the hallway and the other side led to the master bedroom. They walked through, finally they making their way to the bedroom, which was dominated by a huge Cal-king bed, with a brown leather headboard. The covers and pillows in tan, brown and blue.

Sunny walked over to the sliding glass door that led out to the deck that wrapped around the whole house. She stared out at the view of the ocean. She had been quiet since they'd entered the house. He hoped it was nerves versus not liking the rental.

He came up behind her, close enough to feel her heat. She must have felt his too, because she tensed. *Nerves, then.*

"Do you like it?" He said quietly.

"Oh, Gabe it's fantastic!" She turned to look up at him.

"Then why are you so quiet?"

"I'm just nervous I guess." She looked down at the floor, avoiding his eyes.

"Sunny, look at me." He waited until she raised her eyes to his. "We don't have to do anything you don't want to, remember that."

"But I want to…badly." She took a deep fortifying breath, "I guess it's more anxious anticipation, than anything."

He stroked the back of his hand down her face. "Maybe later. Are you hungry?" He wanted to take the focus off of sex and put it back on just enjoying each other.

"Yeah." She relaxed a little with sex taken off the menu.

"Well, we can make something here. The kitchen is fully stocked. Or we can go out to eat." Gabe suggested.

"What's the plan for tonight?" Sunny asked, weighing her options.

"There's a music festival tonight that I want to take you too. And before that I'd like to take you to a nice dinner."

"Alright. Then I think we should stay here and make something. Just the two of us." Sunny said, wanting to enjoy as much alone time with him as possible.

"Good. Well then, go fix me some food wench!" He did his best pirate impersonation and smacked her on the butt, making her yelp and run out the room laughing.

~~~

After they fixed lunch they spent the rest of the afternoon, eating and drinking Mimosas out on the deck. Gabe had asked her more about her childhood and college experiences. He told her stories about working on the different movies he had been in, and even a little more about what it was like living in foster homes.

They were laying intertwined on the couch switching

between making out and flipping through channels on the flatscreen. They were making fun of all the ridiculous reality shows, when Sunny realized it was time to start getting ready for their night out.

She untangled herself from Gabe's limbs. "Alright mister, it's time for me to start getting ready."

"Okay. You take the big bathroom. And I'll use the one off of the spare bedroom." He unfolded his long body from the couch.

She stood on her tiptoes and gave him a quick kiss on the lips. "See you in a little bit."

She went into the master bedroom and opened her overnight bag that he had put on the bed for her. She grabbed her undies, dress, shoes and makeup, and brought them all into the bathroom. She hung the dress on the inside of the door, letting some of the few wrinkles it had gotten in the bag; fall out while she got ready.

She took another quick shower, wanting to be refreshed for the night out. She slipped on her new black lace demi-bra with little hot pink details and the matching lacey boy-shorts. Knowing this was what he would see later tonight, she took the time out to try and see what he might see. Her breasts practically spilled out of the lacey cups, her ass looked ripe, extra plump and firm in the panties. Her tummy was soft and round, sloping down towards her sex. She guessed the image wasn't too unappealing, giving her the little added burst of confidence she needed to get through the night.

The dress she'd chosen for the night was a knee length cocktail dress. The bodice was black with horizontal crisscrossing pleats around the bust. A full skirt with a white background and black, pink, red and blue horizontal stripes of various sizes that wrapped around the skirt and white crinoline underneath to give it a little more poof. All in all, the look was a cross between 'high tea-time' and a 'night on the town'. She loved it.

Sunny finished everything up with her customary eyeliner, mascara and shimmery lip-gloss. She left her wild curls down to frame her face and shoulders. Then she stepped into her pink wedges. She hoped that they wouldn't be walking around too much, or she'd be barefoot before the night was even halfway through. As the finishing touch, she sprayed on her favorite perfume, a light floral fresh-out-of-the-shower smell.

Sunny came out of the bathroom and stepped into the living room, searching for Gabe.

"Sweet Jesus!" She turned to the kitchen where Gabe was standing, holding a forgotten bottle of champagne and staring at her.

He set the bottle down on the counter and walked around the island to stand in front of her, eating her up with his gaze.

"Uh, I changed my mind we're staying in." Gabe proclaimed.

She giggled at his comment, feeling flattered. "No, you promised me a night out. So we're going."

"How can you expect me to look at this view all night *and* expect me to contain myself?" He asked, looking dead serious.

"Like I don't have the same problem." This time it was Sunny's turn to stare him up and down. "You're absolutely gorgeous, Gabe.

He had on nice tailored black slacks, a tucked in white button-down dress shirt, the sleeves rolled up to his elbows and top buttons undone. Along with a fitted gray vest with a loosely knotted black and gray patterned tie, with shiny black dress shoes. His glorious mane of unruly jet-black *McDreamy* waves only slightly maintained, flipped up near his ears and curled at his collar. The look was very much like sexy CEO after a long day at the office. He looked like he'd just stepped off the pages of *GQ*. *I have no words. I have no fucking words!*

"At least if I turn you on no one can tell. But I won't have any such luck." Gabe grumbled.

Looking down, Sunny saw the unmistakable bulge in his slacks. She still couldn't get over the fact that *she* made his body react that way.

Sunny walked around to the kitchen to fill their champagne

flutes. "Here, let's make a toast and drink some bubbly and get out of here to enjoy the night." She was trying to come up with ways to distract them both.

He inhaled deeply through the nose, and then exhaled through his mouth. "Okay, Sweet girl." He held up his glass and she clinked her glass with his. "To an amazing night with a beautiful woman." Then leaning in to whisper in her ear, "Oh, and be sure to keep on those 'come fuck me' heels later."

She instantly blushed.

~~~

He took her to an amazing five-star steakhouse. They dined on juicy steaks and succulent lobster, occasionally feeding forkfuls to each other across the table. Teasing one another, until the sexual tension was at an all-time high and their gazes were heavy-lidded and heated.

Gabe quickly paid the check and they made their way to the Avalon ballroom, where the pulsing beats of the music from the festival could be heard in the distance.

On their way in, Gabe was stopped a few times by fans to sign autographs, though most of the people there were polite and let him have his space. He paid for their admission and guided Sunny through the crowd to the bar. He bought them both beers and brought their drinks over to an empty table.

Looking at a flyer for the event, Sunny noticed that it was a Reggae festival, if the current band didn't give it away. The music, the drums, the couples on the dance floor had a very sexual feel to it. *This should be interesting.* They had just escaped the tension in the romantically set restaurant, only to run straight into the sexual den of reggae delights. *Now I know* 'How Stella Got Her Groove Back'*!*

Sunny chugged her beer down like a drunken frat boy, trying to calm her frayed nerves. Gabe smiled at her impressed. And then he walked back to the bar to get her another beer.

Once he came back, he set her full beer down in front of her.

"Are you trying to get me drunk?" She eyed him suspiciously.

"No. I'm trying to get you relaxed enough to dirty dance with me. Since I get the feeling that you secretly were a Patrick Swayze fan."

"Oh, it's no secret. I *am* a huge Swayze fan. 'No one puts Baby in a corner'!" She winked at him as he laughed.

They both downed the rest of their beers and Gabe pulled her onto the crowded dance floor. The bass and drums combined to pound out a sensual rhythm. Sunny swayed her hips to the beat and Gabe followed. His hands were on her hips and she slid her arms up and around his neck, plunging her fingers into the hair on the nape of his neck. He bent down and pressed his forehead against hers, staring at her a few beats before capturing her lips in a blistering kiss.

Sunny gasped as she pulled away and turned in his arms. She pressed her ass into his steel erection, making him moan in her ear. His lips were on her in an instant, in the space between her neck and shoulder. His tongue flicked out occasionally, to taste her skin leaving, a damp trail in his wake. Her head was thrown back, the curls around her face now wet and plastered to her skin. Her lips parted and gasped as he grinded into her from behind.

They were oblivious to any and everything around them. She reached her arms back to comb through his hair again. And he took advantage of the access that she made and rested his hands on the underside of her breasts. Then he stroked down her sides, all the way to the hem of her dress. He scraped his fingertips up her thighs, exposing the skin as the dress lifted with his hands. Sunny grabbed his wrists, stopping his progress before he exposed too much. He left her panting, wet and desperate for more. She turned to face him again, staring him right in the eyes as she nodded her head. She was ready.

Chapter 10

They stumbled into the beach house after their taxi had
dropped them off. Gabe barely had the door closed before he
slammed Sunny against it, claiming her mouth and grasping
under her ass lifting her off the floor. Instinctively she wrapped
her legs around his waist. With every plunge of his tongue into
her mouth he thrust his hardness against her core. The feeling
was so exquisite, her mouth dropped open unable to hold the kiss,
her cries fanning against his lips.

Gripping her tighter, Gabe walked her back to the bedroom
placing her gently on the bed. He stepped back and stared at her
intently as he started to strip. Sunny wanted to do the honors
herself and feel every inch of skin he revealed, but she couldn't
make herself move. She was entranced by his performance.
'Magic Mike' *who?!*

Once his vest, tie and shoes were off he started on the shirt,
each undone button exposing more hard flesh. The shirt dropped
to the floor, his broad muscled chest rose and fell harshly with his
heavy breathing. His corded shoulders and arms worked as he
undid his belt and pants, which both joined the rest of his clothes
on the floor.

Gabe stood in just his gray boxer-briefs, his erection
straining against the material. As he reached for the waistband,
Sunny's breath hitched in her throat, waiting for the big reveal.
And dear God, big it was. When he stood before her completely
naked, her brain checked out for the night. In the past she had
thought the naked male form was pretty hilarious. She wasn't
laughing now. His body was sculpted art. Even his thighs and

calves were perfectly formed bulging muscles. And the muscle at the apex of his thighs had her swallowing hard.

He was huge! She had never been with anyone that large before. The sight was kind of frightening. The thickness was nearly the circumference of a *Coke* can. And his cock was so long that it jutted up to his bellybutton. *What am I gonna do with all that!*

He must have seen the panic on her face. "Sunny, I promise I won't hurt you." His voice was thick with want.

"I don't see how you couldn't. You're massive. You do realize I'm short and my womb is about the length of my small hand?!" Sunny studied him tensely. *Dammit I'm killing the mood. Just relax and trust him.* "I'm sorry, I'll shut up now."

As big as he was all she wanted to do was taste him. Sliding off the bed, she knelt in front of him. He had that amazingly sexy as hell muscle that went from the sides of his waist to the base of his hardness. She reached up to caress the muscle and he shuddered. Her hands making her way to his manhood, she had to use both hands to even wrap all the way around him. His hands started clenching at his sides. She stroked her tongue over the swollen head, licking up the slit to taste the pre-cum that seeped out.

"Sunny stop, if you keep that up this will be over before it even began." Gabe gasped and pulled away from him, hauling her to her feet.

He plundered her mouth like a starving man, while reaching back to slide down the zipper of her dress. He slid the straps down her shoulders and the dress dropped pooling at her feet. She squeezed her eyes shut as he stepped back to take her in. She heard him draw in his breath sharply and yet she still couldn't open her eyes, afraid to see disgust there.

"Sunny, open your eyes." Gabe commanded softly.

Slowly she looked up at him and there was no disgust, only an all-consuming desire. His index finger traced the skin above her bra. "So beautiful", he whispered. Sliding his hands behind her back, he unclasped her bra easily and slid the straps down her arms, baring her full breasts to the cool air. Her nipples puckered, demanding him to show them attention. His fingertips caressed down her neck, smoothed over her collarbone and finally down to her luscious mounds. He cupped them, caressing the tips with his thumbs. He watched as she bit her lip, restraining her cries.

"Don't hold back, baby. Let me hear you. By the time I'm done I want to hear you screaming my name." He licked at her trembling lips.

Then without warning he swooped down sucking an erect nipple into his mouth. This time she did cry out and her hips thrust forward, seeking contact. His tongue swirled around the peak, and then moved to give the other nipple the same attention. Now that Sunny had found her voice she couldn't stop the little gasps, moans and sighs that escaped her throat. She had never been very vocal during sex, but Gabe gave her the confidence to be herself.

He kissed down her tummy slowly, stopping here, lingering there. Her stomach had always been 'no-man's land'. She had no idea how arousing it could be. Now down on his knees in front of her, Sunny held her breath when Gabe reached her panties, she felt a little self-conscious over how soaking wet her panties were. But once again Gabe shocked the shit out of her by burying his nose in the juncture of her thighs and breathed deeply.

"God, you smell so good." Gabe growled as he yanked her boy-shorts down her legs.

Unsteady in her heels he helped her step out of her panties, his hands wrapped around her ankles and caressed up her thick firm legs. His hands stopped at her ass cheeks, caressing her there. Then he blew cool air softly on her hot wet clit. Her knees buckled and she grasped his shoulders.

"Gabe, please!" Sunny begged him.

"I've got you." He steadied her with his hands on her waist.

He gently laid her back on the bed, with her ass on the edge of the bed and rested her thighs on his shoulders. He stared up at her as he licked his lips, ready to dive in.

"Gabe, wait." Sunny sat up and pressed against his

shoulders, stopping him. "You don't have to do that."

Gabe gave her a stern look and opened his mouth to say something, but she stopped him.

"It's just that…well…I've never gotten 'there' from oral or actual sex for that matter. But I want that connection with you, so we can skip this part if you want."

Gabe got up from his crouched position between her thighs and crawled up her body like a predator stalking its prey. "Sunny, first off I'm sorry that no man cared enough to find what makes you come. And second, part of the reason you can't is because you're too much in your own head. Stop thinking and just *feel*. Now…no more interruptions." He crawled back down her body, kissing along the way and reigniting the flames that had cooled during her neurosis.

Back between her thighs, Gabe kissed the top of her smooth hairless mound as his index finger skated over her slick labia. His finger slid inside her wetness, crooking his finger to hit the soft tissue inside that made her hips rise off the bed. The first touch of his tongue flicking her clit made her gasp and buck against his mouth. He groaned and covered her clit with his mouth, making figure eights on the sensitive nub. She was so aroused that her wetness started to run down his hand, and he slid his finger out and licked up her slit, lapping up her sweet essence. Sunny felt her climax building deep in her gut, her breath rushed out in desperate pants. Her hands reached out to grab his hair, not knowing whether to pull his mouth away or push him closer. Gabe sensing her impending release, latched on to her throbbing clit, sucking it into his mouth and flicked it once. And Sunny exploded, losing absolute control.

"Gabe!" She screamed his name as she fucked his face. "Ahh…God!" She cried out.

Her pussy flooded with her come and he lapped up every drop. Gabe continued to torture her with his tongue until she couldn't take anymore and scooted up the bed trying to get away from him.

"No more!" She panted, skin flushed.

"I knew you'd be all hot pink on the inside." He said crawling up her body once more.

She glimpsed his massive erection that was an angry purple color as it slid up her body. She was amazed at his restraint.

He glided up her body, stopping to flick each nipple with his tongue, amazingly already rekindling her need for him. Gabe kissed up her neck to her jaw, and then crushed his mouth to hers. She tasted herself on his tongue and moaned into his mouth. He rubbed his satiny steel against her labia, while licking and biting her bottom lip.

"I know we should've talked about this before now, but are you on birth control?" He asked the muscles in his jaw flexing as he tried to hold back.

"Yes...since my last relationship. Ah..." Sunny gasped as the tip of his manhood slid across her clit. "And I've been tested. I'm clean."

"I trust you. So am I. I've never not used a condom, but I don't want any barriers between us. I want to feel your heat, your wetness." Gabe said as his arms trembled with need as he hovered at her entrance.

She nodded, unable to speak. He reached down and positioned the head of his cock at her opening. He teased her, dipping the tip shallowly into her warmth. Her hips came off the bed trying to get closer, wanting him deeper.

"Please..." she moaned into his mouth.

Gabe grasped her hips and plunged in to the hilt. They both threw their heads back as he hit the top of her womb.

"Aaaahhhh..." she cried.

"Shiiit!" His head dropped to the crook of her neck.

Threading her fingers in his thick hair, she held on for dear life as he pummeled her with deep thrusts. He stretched her to capacity, pain intermingling with pleasure, creating an indescribable feeling.

"God Sunny, you're so tight. You feel so...good." He groaned into her hair.

Rising up, he knelt between her legs, bringing them up to

rest against his chest. Her heels bracketed his head. The sight was incredibly arousing. The position brought him even deeper than she could've believed possible. He started pumping into her, swiveling his hips and caressing up and down her legs. Sunny started to feel the tingling deep in her core again, but stronger than before. There was no way she was going to survive this one.

"No no, Gabe. I can't!" She started to panic, never feeling this sensation before.

"Yes…you can. You will." Gabe growled, holding on tighter to her.

He reached down to glide his thumb over her clit at the same time as he rotated his hips, thrusting into her. And she lost it. Her legs began to shake and her back arched off of the mattress.

"GABE!" Sunny screamed his name as tears streamed down the sides of her face.

Her body was racked with shutters as her walls clenched around his thrusting cock, causing him to explode inside of her.

"Sunny…FUCK!" He yelled as he thrust harder through his climax, her pussy milking every drop from him.

He collapsed on top of her, their damp skin sliding together and his weight on her was comforting as she came apart.

"Aw baby, don't cry." Gabe kissed the tears that spilled down her temples and cheeks.

She couldn't even respond, just covered her eyes with one hand trying to turn her face away from him.

"Baby, why are you crying?" Gabe's voice was thick with concern. He pulled her hand away from her face. "Look at me, please."

Heartbreaking honey-brown eyes looked at him. "It's stupid and cheesy."

"Nothing you say is stupid. Talk to me. You're making me think I did something wrong." Gabe rolled to the side breaking their bodies' intimate connection, slid her up against him and rested her head in the crook of his arm and chest.

"It was just…the most amazing beautiful moment of my life. I've never had or felt that before. And when I finally did stop thinking and started feeling, I think the floodgates opened. And now I'm just feeling everything." She inhaled and exhaled slowly calming herself down as Gabe rubbed up and down her arm soothingly.

"Sunny, what just happened between us isn't the norm. I've never had that either. Hell, I never even thought it was possible." He turned her face towards his, forcing her to look at him. "I…I'm totally falling in love with you Madison Stone. God…I've never said that to anyone before." His intense blue eyes gazed at her with adoration.

Her eyes filled with tears again. "I love you Gabriel, but how does that make any sense? We just met a week and a half ago."

"It doesn't have to make sense. There are no definite rules or guidelines to love and relationships. Each couple does what's right for them. They write their own story."

"So…we make our own story?" Sunny tried to squash down her worries.

"Yes." Gabe quickly rolled on top of her, taking her by surprise, especially considering the hardness she felt against her thigh. "Now…say it again." He grinned down at her.

Sunny knew she could've played dumb and acted like she didn't know what he was asking, but she also knew that this man craved love. Nearly thirty-eight years without it was too long. So at the risk of heartbreak, she gave it freely.

"I love you." She said softly.

"And I love you, Sunny."

Without hesitation, he slowly entered her. She didn't think she'd be ready for round two yet, but her body thought differently. He rested his weight on his forearms, his hands held her face and his eyes held her gaze as he started to thrust into her.

Their second time was different. There was no rush this time. He savored her, enjoyed her heat and wetness as she enveloped him. He watched every nuance of emotion that flickered across her face as he pumped into her. She started to close her eyes, but he refused to relinquish eye-contact.

"Sunny, look at me. Keep your eyes open, Sweet Girl. I need

to see you."

His speed picked up, feeling his climax just beneath the surface. Sunny's face telling him that she was also close. So he swirled his hips knowing that it would set her off. He felt her muscles flutter around him and her gasps grew louder. Her eyelids drifted lower, as if she'd close her eyes.

"No Sunny. I need to watch you come."

His words must have set her off. Her eyes widened and she cried out. Her walls flexed convulsively against his cock drawing out his orgasm and he erupted, spilling his seed inside of her again. She writhed beneath him as he continued to thrust into her lengthening both their orgasms until they were both spent. He collapsed and pulled Sunny to him, spooning her from behind as they fell asleep.

Chapter 11

Sunny woke up to sunlight streaming in through the windows and strong arms slipping around her. One around her waist and the other across her chest holding her tight, and her naked back flush against a solid bare chest. She stretched like a cat, feeling a delicious soreness in her limbs and nether regions reminding her of the previous night. She smiled and opened her eyes. Sitting on the bed in front of her was a tray of food. There was a plate with an omelet and bacon, a little saucer with buttered toast, a bowl of fresh fruit and a glass of orange juice. *What the…?!*

Sunny's head whipped around to see a very happy masculine face, smiling down at her.

"Good morning, Sweet Girl. God, it feels like I've waited a lifetime to say that to you face to face in bed." He was literally grinning from ear to ear.

"That's for me?" Sunny asked unsure, glancing over at the tray of food.

"Yes."

"And you made all that?"

"Yes."

"Well…bend me over, smack my ass and call me Irish," Sunny deadpanned.

Gabe fell back with a deep belly laugh, clutching his rock hard abs. "Maybe we'll try that later." He said after he got his laughter under control.

Gabe watched her as she pinched the skin of her forearm. "What are you doing?" He looked at her amused.

"Just checking to make sure I'm awake. Seriously Gabe, this shit just doesn't happen to me. You made me breakfast in bed for God's sake! My usual fare is: guys letting the door close in my face when walking into a building or better yet, holding my apartment door open for a guy while my hands are filled with heavy grocery bags and not even getting a 'thank you'! I thought the word 'chivalry' and been removed from the English dictionary." Sunny said in shocked awe.

Gabe leaned in and kissed her lush lips passionately, and then released her just as quickly. "Then I think it's high time that you're treated like the queen you are. And I'm just the man to do it. Now, eat up before your breakfast gets cold."

"Uh…maybe you should wait until I've brushed my teeth before you go kissing me like that." Sunny grinned as she sat back against the pillows.

"I like your morning breath", he kissed her again, before placing the tray on her lap.

"Ew! So, did you eat anything yet?"

"Yeah, while you were sleeping."

"Man, you must have really worn me out, if I slept that hard!" She gave him a sassy smile.

"I do what I can." He smiled back. "So how about I run a bath for us while you're eating?"

"Okay." She responded shyly.

He got up and walked into the bathroom while Sunny tried to eat. She wasn't feeling very hungry, but then again that could be because the butterflies in her stomach weren't making much room for food. Though she did end up eating a little bit of everything, seeing as how he had went through so much trouble to make her breakfast. And surprisingly, everything was delicious. He was a good cook.

She heard Gabe shutting the water off as she placed the tray on the nightstand and wrapped the top sheet around her naked body. She grabbed some bobby-pins out of her purse and twisted her mass of curls up and out of the way for their bath. Then she padded to the bathroom quietly and leaned against the doorway, watching him pour oil that smelled like lavender into the steaming water and swirling it around.

Sensing her presence, he turned to look at her. They quietly studied each other for a moment, him wearing nothing but jeans that hung low on his hips and ass like sin and her wrapped in nothing but a sheet.

"Well don't you make a vision?" Gabe strolled over to her, kissed her lips and guided her further into the bathroom.

Gabe watched her brush her teeth, clutching the sheet to her body the entire time. He knew she was still self-conscious about her body. And he was sure the bright light of day made it worse. When she was finished, she turned back to him. She reached out to undo his jeans, and pushed them over his hips letting them fall to the floor. He was already fully aroused. The sight made her flush all over.

He removed her hand from the sheet and unwrapped her like a present, the sheet fell to the floor with his jeans, leaving her bare. He made an appreciative sound in the back of his throat, trying to convey his fascination with her body. Then he swooped down to pick her up, cradling her against his hard body as he swung her legs over the edge of the tub. He eased her legs down to stand in the tub and she lowered herself into the warm fragrant water, scooting forward to give him room to get in behind her.

Once in, he immediately pulled her closer between his legs, his erection resting against her lower back and her top half against his chest. They both sighed at the same time, making them both laugh at each other.

"So is there anything that you want to do today, before we have to leave?" Gabe asked as he entwined their wet fingers together.

"I'd say, stay right here in this tub, but then we'd get all prune-y."

"How about this: we make love, then walk on the beach, then make love, then eat a late lunch, make love again and then head back?"

"Sounds like a plan to me." Sunny chuckled at his

suggestion.

"Good."

Gabe soaked a washcloth in the water then gently squeezed it onto Sunny's skin; letting the water run down her neck, shoulders and breasts. He grabbed the bar of soap from the ledge of the tub, rubbing it between his hands.

Starting at her neck, he massaged the lather into her skin, moving slowly down to work her creamy brown shoulders. She bent forward giving him better access to her back. Getting the hint, he worked his way down kneading her muscles along the way. Finished with her back, he brought her back to his chest, re-soaped his hands and slid them down to her breasts. Gliding his hands over and under, gently squeezing them as he stroked up until he pinched the tips with light pressure. Her moans turned into gasps, her lower half started to move restlessly. His hands journeyed down her rounded tummy, making his way to her wet pussy. The slickness of her arousal felt differently than the wetness of the water. His fingers sought her clit between her labia. Making contact, she cried out, arched her back and dug her nails into his thighs. Sunny tried closing her legs, but Gabe lifted his ankles over hers forcing her legs to spread apart.

He continued to play her like an instrument, her cries practically making him come it was such a turn-on. Now that she was learning to relax and enjoy pleasure, her natural sensuality was breathtaking.

Gabe palmed her wet heat, sliding two fingers inside and using his thumb to strum her clit. She pumped her hips into one hand, while his other stroked her breasts and nipples. Her body bowed and tensed, her insides the only thing moving as her muscles contracted against his fingers, crying out her release.

Her orgasm fading, she went limp and collapsed onto his chest. As her breathing calmed Gabe whispered in her ear, "Turn around, Sweet Girl."

Gabe helped her onto his lap as she turned. Her knees on either side of him, she raised her hips to hover over his hardness. Positioning him at her entrance, she slammed down onto his awaiting cock. The sudden shock of being inside her tight heat again, made him shout out her name. Sunny sat still for a moment letting the sensation envelope them. Then she started to move, raising her hips as she clenched her muscles around him, only to slam back down again. She continued the slow torture and Gabe practically went cross-eyed from the feeling.

He leaned forward drawing one of her wet slippery nipples into his mouth. Her head was thrown back and eyes closed, enjoying the control she had over him as she rode him. Taking the control back before he lost his mind, Gabe grasped her hips and started pounding into her at a ridiculous speed. As she pushed down, he pumped up, matching her thrust for thrust. The water splashed over the edge every time their bodies slapped together.

"Ah…Gabe! I'm gonna come again!" Sunny cried out.

She convulsed around him and her scream shattered his ears. Again her contracting walls instantly made him come. His cock pulsated into her as he reached his climax.

"FUCK!" He yelled out, as he gripped her hips tightly continuing to pump into her.

Finally wrung out, his head fell back on the tub and she sprawled across him. She nuzzled her face into his neck, sighing tiredly.

They sat in the cooling water for a while longer, holding on to each other tightly. Realizing they were starting to prune and she was shivering from the now cool water, Gabe sat up and Sunny looked up at him sleepily.

"We better finish washing and get out of this water." He suggested softly.

"Mmm…" Was all she could get out.

He made her stand as he finished washing her lower half, moving quickly because of the cool air making her quiver. Then she took the soap from him and washed his body, being quite thorough in certain areas, making his body start to come alive again.

"Uh, you're asking for trouble Sweet Girl." He said in a

warning tone.

"Oops, sorry." She said making a guilty face.

She finished washing him and after they were rinsed off, he stepped out of the tub first and then lifted her out. He grabbed a gigantic fluffy towel and vigorously dried her off, trying to generate warmth back into her body. And she did the same for him. The whole process was sweet and loving and warmed both their hearts.

"Okay, now that we've checked one of our plans off the list, we should probably get dressed and move on to the next. Before I skip the walk on the beach and move right into making love again." Gabe grinned devilishly at her.

Sunny just grinned back at him as she made her way into the bedroom to lotion down her body and get dressed. Which they found didn't work out so great, since he completely ravished her after watching her apply the cream to her luscious curves. Sunny filed that information in the back of her mind. *Note to self: Don't lotion in front of Gabe if we have plans to be somewhere.* Needless to say, the walk on the beach came way later.

~~~

Sunny and Gabe spent the rest of the day enjoying each other. They walked along the beach holding hands, making lunch together, and making love on and off.

As they packed up to leave, Gabe noticed that Sunny slipped more and more into a melancholy mood. He was feeling a little morose himself, knowing that their idyllic weekend would soon be coming to an end. At this point he was ready to march over to her apartment, pack up all her stuff and move her into his home in Malibu.

But he knew that she wasn't ready for that step. Exchanging 'I love yous' had already scared the shit out of her. He couldn't have been more thrilled. She was everything that he could've ever wanted, didn't even know he wanted. He felt so…full. No one had ever loved him before, which made him guard his heart, not willing to love anyone else either. And now that he had her, he wouldn't let her go. He didn't think he could, even if he tried.

He knew that she probably wouldn't be freaking out if he was some regular guy working construction or something like that. His career, his fame was the problem. But there was nothing he could do about that. All he could do was try to guide her through the life of scrutiny he had thrown her into and hope she could make it out the other side unscathed.

So with a heavy heart, he grabbed their bags and led her out of the beach house. She was quiet the whole way back, just leaning into him as he drove the boat back to Long Beach.

Once there, he called a cab to pick them up. He wanted to ride with her back to her apartment to make sure she got there safely. Then he'd take the cab back to the boat to take it back to Malibu.

Sunny finally spoke, once they were in the cab. "You didn't have to come with me, only for you to have to come right back."

"It's nothing. I had to make sure you got home safe." He brushed her hair away from her face.

She just nodded and remained quiet for the rest of the short ride.

When the cab pulled up to her building, Gabe told the cabbie to keep the meter running. Then he walked Sunny into her building and to her door. He held her face in both hands and leaned in to kiss her thoroughly. He broke away and rested his forehead on hers, breathing deeply to calm his pulse.

"I'd come in, but then I'd never leave. And I have to get my boat back, since it's only temporary docking."

"I know." Sunny said sadly.

"Please Sunny, stop being so sad. It's not the end of the world because the weekend is over." Concern was written all over his face.

"I know. I know. It's just that it was the best weekend of my life and I don't want it to be over. Reality is totally overrated!" She huffed indignantly.

He chuckled, "Oh, this weekend was nothing but real. I can

still smell you, taste you on my tongue, and feel your warmth around my cock. So it was very real for me."

"Well since you put it that way…" She said in a shaky voice.

"So…lunch sometime this week?" Gabe changed the subject before he took her in the middle of her public hallway.

"Yes, please. Since it's the beginning of a new week and I have to work this weekend I'm off Tuesday."

"Then how about you spend the day with me on the set? Watch me work?"

"I'd love that!" The happy-go-lucky Sunny he knew made an reappearance.

"And you've already gotten Friday off for the premiere, right?"

"Yes."

"Good. I'll call you when I get home, to let you know I made it safely."

"Alright. Be careful, Gabe."

"I will. Oh, and Sunny?"

"Yes?"

"I'll wait right here while you get me your screenplays." He smiled at her, knowing she had hoped he'd forget. She gave him a nervous scowl and walked into her apartment.

"Here. This is the flashdrive with all my work on it, and this is my notebook with more notes on each one. The notes are titled." She said once she'd come back to the door with the items.

"Thank you." He knew showing him her work took a lot of courage on her part.

He leaned in once more and kissed her softly on the lips, keeping it chaste so he wouldn't be tempted to stay. Leaving her was already hard enough.

Chapter 12

Sunny woke up Monday morning, way too early for her tastes. But it had been a restless night, so when she woke up for the fifth time, she decided to just stay up.

So with plenty of time to kill, she decided to make a cup of coffee and check her *Facebook*. She hadn't been on her page since she'd met Gabe, not wanting to be tempted to post something about her new relationship. She still doubted her ability to hold onto the most sought after man in the country.

Opening her laptop, she brought up her browser. Her main page popped up with the latest news stories and before she could click on her 'favorites' a headline caught her eye.

"OH MY GOD!" She said to herself.

There in the middle of the screen was a still shot of her and Gabe on a crowded dance floor, with a headline that read: *GABRIEL WOLF HEATS UP THE DANCE FLOOR WITH A LITTLE HOT COCOA-click to watch video.*

"Fuck my life!" Sunny shouted into her empty apartment. "Can we not do anything, without it being recorded for fucking prosperity?!"

Sunny stared at the screen for a few minutes, debating watching the video. Unfortunately, curiosity got the best of her and she clicked on the link. The website with the video loaded and then she clicked play. Before her eyes, she watched the sexually charged moment between herself and Gabe. Even a blind man could see the passion and tension between them, so she knew everyone else would too. Oh, God! She hoped her parents wouldn't watch it, but she was pretty sure this would make it to

E!, *TMZ*, *EXTRA*, and *ACCESS HOLLYWOOD. Ladies and gentlemen, we would like to present Dirty Dancing: Catalina Nights!*

Sunny picked up her phone to text Gabe. She hoped that he was already up.

Sunny: *Gabe please call me as soon as you can.*

Her phone rang within seconds of sending the text. She answered immediately.

"Hey." She said trying to control her shaking voice.

"Sunny! What's wrong?" She could tell that he was panicked.

"There's a video of us that just went viral." She said quietly.

"What?! Fuck! A video of us doing what?" Gabe growled into the phone.

"Of us dancing at the music festival. And if you remember that dance as well as I do, even before I watched the video, you'll know that that was an intense moment. And it totally came across on camera. If it wasn't so public and embarrassing, I'd say it was smoking hot. But knowing the whole world is going to see it…I might as well walk around naked, that's how exposed I feel." She finished her tirade in a huff.

"Sunny, please don't let this get to you. Eventually it will all die down. They'll get bored and move on to stalking someone else. But I can tell you what will speed up that process…"

"What?"

"Letting the media know we're together and not just as some fling. The more we hide from them, the more they'll hound us." Gabe's voice had an anxious tone to it.

"You know, I think you're right. It's kinda like the Madonna-effect." Sunny said perking up a little.

"What's the Madonna-effect?" Gabe tried to contain his chuckle.

"Well I just made up the name. But I always thought she was a genius back in the day. She was just totally up front about the fact that she was a freak. You know, with the *Truth or Dare*

~ 131 ~

movie and all that. It gave the media nothing to write about, because she'd already put it out there."

"Exactly! So Friday at the premiere will be our first night out in front of the media and I'm going to put this shit to rest. I don't like the way all this makes you feel." Sunny could sense his worry.

"Well hearing your voice and talking it out with you, always makes me feel better." Sunny smiled into the phone.

"Good, I'm glad."

~~~

Gabe was already on the set in his trailer when Sunny had text him. She'd nearly given him a heart attack, she never texted him first or this early. But now that the situation was under control, the first thing he did after he got off the phone with her was look up the video on his tablet.

Shit! She was right, it was fucking hot as hell. He was getting hard just watching it, remembering the anticipation he felt in that moment of eventually making love to her. But he could understand why she had been upset. Even though they had been in a public setting, their intimate moment was not something for the world to see.

Gabe shook his head as he backed out of the website. *Do these people understand that they're literally fucking up my love life?!* He sat the tablet down on the table and headed out the trailer to start the day. All of the cast and crew that were scheduled for the day were outside waiting for the morning meeting to start. And there in the middle was Josiah with a snide look on his face, like he was waiting for Gabe to show up.

"Hey, Gabe."

"Josiah." Gabe nodded his head to the actor, prepared to ignore him. He found that wasn't so easy.

"Man, I never really thought about hooking up with a black chick before, but you've made me rethink things. She really is one hot plump piece of ass." Josiah said loud enough for almost everyone to hear.

The various conversations died down, and it was so quiet Gabe could hear a pin drop. Not that he would've heard it anyway, with the roar of blinding rage in his ears. Before anyone realized what was about to happen, Gabe took two steps forward and dropped Josiah like a ton of bricks when he clocked him in the face with a clenched fist.

Everyone gasped and rushed forward. Some to hold back Gabe from beating the shit out of Josiah further, and some to help Josiah who was rolling around on the ground.

"You broke my fucking nose, asshole!" Josiah screamed through the blood pouring from his face.

Kyle, who rarely ever raised his voice, got in Josiah's face. "Shut the fuck up Josiah, before I let him beat the shit out of you! What you said was uncalled for and you deserve more than a bloody nose. You're not that big a star yet, a few words from this cast and crew and the only work you'll be able to get in this town are *Viagra* commercials."

Kyle motioned over the set paramedic, and then he walked over to Gabe.

"I'm sorry man. I just kinda lost it." Gabe shook his head frowning.

"Don't worry about it. You need someone to look at that hand." Kyle said, looking down at the hand that Gabe was flexing unconsciously.

"Naw, I'm good." Gabe looked down at his swelling knuckles, trying to figure out how he was going to hide them from Sunny.

"Well at least put some ice on it." Kyle paused, thinking for a moment. "Gabe, you're going to have to figure out how to control your temper when it comes to Sunny. It's great that you're protective of her, but you can't fight everyone. And I just don't want to see you getting smacked with a ton of lawsuits." Kyle said with genuine concern.

"God, I know. I'm just so afraid of losing her because of all this." Gabe gestured around the set and the paparazzi at the gate in the distance.

"Don't worry man. I'm sure everything will be fine." He patted Gabe on the back and walked away.

Gabe wasn't so sure anymore.

~~~

"Woo honey! That was one crazy hot video! I'm so jealous!" Sunny cringed as Santiago came up to her while she was checking inventory in the back room with a few others.

So far no one had seemed to have seen the video and Sunny had thought she was in the clear. Now thanks to Santiago a few ears pricked at the new gossip, especially Becca's.

"Ooh what?! What happened?" Becca begged Santiago.

"Santiago, please don't start. I don't need everyone in my business." Sunny begged for a whole different reason.

"Honey, how could you not want to share what it's like to be with a mega famous celebrity? And you've been with him, right? Because girl, that video said it all!" Santiago said, looking her up and down knowingly.

"Oh now I've got to know what's going on!" Becca bounced up and down pulling on Santiago's arm.

"Don't worry, I already have it up and ready on my phone to show you." Santiago ignored Sunny's scowl.

Swiping the screen on his phone, Santiago did indeed have the video ready to go. Sunny walked away from them to finish what she was working on, trying to calm her fury. But it was hard when she could hear the reggae music from that night blaring out from his phone and the loud gasps of Becca.

Sunny had had enough when she heard the video start again and looked over to see Santiago and Becca watching it again with another co-worker. At this point everyone would know before the hour was up. She stormed out of the backroom to the front of the store, more willing to deal with grumpy customers than her so-called friends.

But that didn't stop them. Becca came running up to her.

"Please Sunny, tell me what it was like to be with him. He is so gorgeous and *big*! Is he big everywhere? You have to tell me!" Becca pleaded with her.

"You know what Becca, I don't have to tell you a goddamned thing!" Sunny hissed under her breath, finally having enough.

"Oh, so it's like that? You get with a big movie star and now you're too good for your friends?!" Becca gave her a look of disgust.

"I just don't like my life on display for the whole world to judge. And I have no idea if what we have is even going to go anywhere, so why would I boast about something that may be over tomorrow?" Sunny gestured wildly before dropping her arms at her sides in defeat.

"Well duh! He's a superstar who dates models and can have anyone he wants. Of course you're just a fling, he's not really gonna marry you or anything. So you enjoy it while it lasts and have great stories to tell in the process." Becca gave her a hateful look.

"Go fuck yourself, Becca." Sunny stomped away angrily, tears welling in her eyes but not wanting Becca to see them.

After that, everyone avoided Sunny like she was a leper. Every now and again she received curious looks from those not very close to her and dirty looks from her friends. *Some friends. Thank God I'm off again tomorrow.* She wasn't sure how much more of this she could take. Her whole life was being turned upside down in the best and worst ways.

~~~

The next morning Sunny dressed for her day on a real movie set. She wore her favorite long white Spanish style peasant skirt and an 80's style off the shoulder coral t-shirt. She paired them with her colorful ankle band sandals, silver hoop earrings and a long necklace. And she pinned up her hair in a pile of curls.

She headed outside when Gabe called to let her know he was

waiting for her out front. The ever familiar butterflies started in her stomach as she walked outside, which turned into the full-blown bats when she saw him for the first time since the weekend. It had only been a day, but it had felt like forever.

He must have missed her too, because he met her halfway, grabbed her face in his hands and kissed her silly before walking her to the truck and opening the door for her. As she got in, she noticed various men scattered here and there with cameras that had huge lens, across the street snapping pictures. Sunny was looking back at them when Gabe slid into the driver's side.

"Don't pay attention to them, Sunny." Gabe looked at her apprehensively.

"They know where I live Gabe!" She threw her hands up in frustration.

"And I'm so sorry for that. But please don't let this come between us." He reached out to clasp her hand in his and squeezed tight.

She squeezed his hand back reassuringly. "I'll try Gabe. But you have to understand that I'm not used to this, and there are going to be times that I freak out. I just need time to adjust, I guess."

"Alright, I'll try not to freak out when you freak out. One freak out at a time. Got it." He winked at her.

"Exactly. So anyway, I can't wait to see you in action today." She put her worries aside and smiled brightly at him.

"Hopefully I'll be able to concentrate. I've never had someone I care about watching me before." He actually looked at her shyly.

They were having so many firsts, not just her, but both of them. It seemed to put them on a level playing field for once.

"So I read your stuff." Gabe said and she nervously looked at him waiting for his thoughts. "They're *great* Sunny. I love the animated movie script. *Disney* or *Pixar* would be perfect studios for that one. And your romantic comedy has a lot of heart and a nice spin on the classic rom-com script formula that is overdone." He reached over and grabbed her hand, giving it a reassuring squeeze. "It only confirmed what I already knew…you're extremely talented Sunny."

Sunny glowed with his praise. "Thanks Gabe, that means a lot coming from you."

"You're welcome, and I'll get them in the right hands a.s.a.p." He grinned at her.

He parked the truck on a residential street. They were filming at a pretty California bungalow today, which posed as the main characters' home, so most of the street was blocked off. Equipment, trailers and people crowded the closed off area. Sunny was bursting with excitement to be able to watch the whole process.

"Come this way. I have a surprise for you." A mischievous look crossed Gabe's face.

"Uh…okay." Sunny looked at him suspiciously.

They walked a little further and then Gabe placed a hand over her eyes, telling her not to peek. Their steps were awkward as he walked her forward with his hand over her face. Then he stopped.

"Are you ready?" He whispered in her ear.

"Uh huh." She nodded.

He lifted his hand away from her eyes. Her pupils took a moment to adjust to the sunlight. And there in front of her was a director's chair with her name 'Madison Stone' and 'Screen Writer' underneath, embossed on the back.

She clapped her hands over her mouth and just stared a moment. She slowly walked forward, then around the chair. Gabe watched her, waiting for a reaction. And a few of the crew members were watching, smiling.

"I can't believe you did this. It's incredible." Sunny said quietly, reaching out to lightly touch her name on the back of the chair, as if it would disappear.

"So you like it?" Gabe smiled like a hopeful little boy.

"Like it? I love it! It's freakin awesome and unbelievably thoughtful." Sunny looked up at him, her honey brown eyes warm and soft.

It was his first gift to her. Sunny's excitement burst fully and she ran to him. He swept her up in his arms and her legs wrapped around his waist. She started kissing him all over his face, making him chuckle. The cast and crew that had been watching and some that had just walked up, started laughing as well.

"It's for you to sit in and watch me today. To feel a part of the crew. And of course to take home and inspire you to write more scripts."

"I love you." She said softly against his lips.

"I love you too, Sweet Girl."

Then Sunny jumped down and skipped to her chair, ready to begin the day.

Chapter 13

Gabe couldn't have been more ecstatic over the way the day was going. Sunny adored her chair that he'd gotten made for her. She sat in it next to Kyle, while he explained the filming process to her and letting her occasionally yell out 'cut' or 'action'. She was in her element, smiling brightly and animatedly talking to everyone. She had the film crew wrapped around her finger and it wasn't even lunch yet. And best of all, Josiah wasn't in any of the scenes so he wasn't on the set stirring up trouble.

Gabe's performances during each take were the best he'd ever done. He'd wanted to make her proud, and she gave him back the passion that he had lost in the last couple of years. It was hard to emote feelings of love, anger, passion and heartbreak when he felt dead inside.

After having Sunny yell 'cut' again, Kyle announced a lunch break. Gabe walked over to Sunny, who was watching the playback of the last take. When he stood in front of her she looked up at him, smiling so hard her cheeks had a rosy tint to them. His heart clenched.

"Hey beautiful, are you hungry?" Gabe asked her.

"Yes and no." At his perplexed look, she explained. "I know I should eat because I haven't had anything in hours, but I'm so hyped up that I don't think I'd be able to eat anything."

"Well I'm starving. So let's get some food from the truck and you can try to eat a little something." He held his hand out to her.

As they walked towards the food truck, she looked back lovingly at her chair.

"No one's going to mess with your chair. Not if I have anything to do about it." His eyes were dancing with laughter at her look of longing.

"I know I just wanna take it with me everywhere." She said unashamed.

"Hmm…I think you love that chair more than me." Gabe gave her a fake scowl.

"Not even close, but someone I love did give it to me, which means it should be cherished." She said with her heart in her eyes.

She left him speechless and a little lump formed in his throat, but he just stepped up to the truck to order their food, giving him some time to pull it together.

Gabe got a gourmet burger with fries and Sunny asked for a Greek salad with chicken. They ate at one of the picnic tables. Gabe inhaled his food, rushing to get some alone time with her in his trailer. She picked at her salad while enthusiastically talking about all she had learned so far.

Once they were done, without a word Gabe quietly got up threw away their plates, grabbed her hand and pulled her from the table, walking her towards his trailer. He let her in first and then stepped in behind her, closing and locking the door firmly.

He still hadn't spoken yet, which he could tell was making her nervous. He took her hand and led her to the stationary dining table, lifted her up to sit on it and then sat in the chair in front of her. She looked down at him curiously.

"And now it's time for dessert." He said smoothly as he started to draw her skirt up her legs.

"Gabe…anyone could pass by and hear. This trailer's walls aren't exactly sound proof." Sunny looked around anxiously.

"Then I suggest you try to keep it down." Gabe gazed at her intently.

"Yeah right, like that's possible with you involved." Sunny said doubtful.

Sunny tried to stop his hands from lifting her skirt further, but she was no match for his strength. And she didn't want to be, craving his touch too much.

So letting him take control, he made her lie back across the table, finished lifting her skirt and his fingers gently skated around the skin that met her panty line grasping the lacy edge, he skimmed them down her legs.

He dropped the pretty panties to the floor and lifted her legs to rest on his shoulders. Her breathing became harsh, anticipating what he was about to do to her.

"I love how wet you already are for me." He murmured as he slid his finger down her damp opening.

"Always." She whimpered.

He placed his tongue on her sweet and savory entrance, sweeping up to her sensitive bud. She cried out loudly, and then clamped a hand over her mouth, probably remembering where they were. The other hand reached down to grip his hair. The sharp tug of pain urged him on, knowing he was the cause of her losing control.

He continued to tease, withholding what she really wanted. Licking softly up her cleft, a quick flick at her clit and then retreating. He built her up, never staying long enough, denying her climax. She tried pumping her hips up and down to get his wet tongue where she wanted it. Her little gasps behind her hand becoming more urgent. He loved it, making her feminine nectar continually flow onto his taste buds. He knew the prolonged torment would build her orgasm to a new level.

Sunny's frustration finally broke her control. She gave up on trying to stifle her noises, not caring who heard her, in her need for release. She uncovered her mouth, clasped his hair in a death-grip with both hands, tilted his face to the position that she wanted it and proceeded to buck against his tongue with wild abandon. Sunny's cries bounced off the thin walls of the trailer. All he could do was hold on for the ride. She was magnificent.

"Aahhh…oh God…oh God…Gabe please…please…*please*!" She wailed as he groaned into her wet heat.

Grabbing hold of her hips, trying to subdue her wild

movements, Gabe latched onto her clit. Sucking it into his mouth and giving the nub one final flick and she exploded on his tongue. She screamed his name so loud that he waited for dogs to start howling in response. He knew she'd be mortified later, but in the moment it was hot as fuck.

He lapped up all of her honeyed milk and then lightly kissed her hairless mound. She sat up on the table covering her beet red face with both hands. He drew her into his arms, stroking her back.

"Don't be ashamed, Sweet Girl. That was beautiful, and so hot that I can barely move from the pain of my ridiculous hard-on." He said and then kissed her damp temple.

"Good. Now it's your turn. I'm not going to be the only one making a fool outta themselves." She said indignantly.

She jumped down off the table, grabbed him by the front of his shirt, he let her lift him out of the chair and then she turned him and pushed him down onto the couch. She slid down to her knees between his legs. Then she made quick work of his belt, unbuttoned his pants and lowered the zipper. She pulled the waistbands to his jeans and boxer-briefs down his hips, until his monster erection was freed. *'Release the Kraken'!*

Sunny didn't hesitate, she licked up his shaft like a *Popsicle*, finishing off by lapping up the fluid collected at the tip. His blood pounded in his ears and he groaned at the sensations her wet tongue and lush lips were giving him.

She swirled her tongue around the purple head. He didn't know how she would be able to fit any of him in her small mouth, but he waited with bated breath, his chest rising and falling with the effort to breathe. She spread her plump lips and plunged down the length of him, as far as she could go. Only making it about a quarter of the way down, but it was enough to make him bark out a cry of pleasure.

Gabe's hands made their way into Sunny's messy curls. Not trying to force her further, but for the need to hold on to something. She slid her hands up to stroke him where her mouth couldn't go. Sunny bobbed her head and made matching rotating strokes up and down his thick shaft.

"Shit Sunny! That feels so fucking good." Gabe shouted out.

His encouragement made her pick up the pace. He watched her little mouth devour him and his heavy sac tightened with the need of relief.

"Ah Sunny, stop! I'm gonna come, you don't have to…" He tried pulling away from her.

Sunny held on tighter and when she looked up at him with loving determination in her eyes as she feasted on him, he lost all control.

"Ah God…SUNNY!" Gabe roared out as he burst in her mouth.

She swallowed everything he had to give, groaning in delight over the pleasure she gave him. And for the first time in his life, Gabe stayed rock hard, as if he hadn't just came. He pulled her up and tossed her on her hands and knees on the couch as if she weighed nothing. Flipping up her skirt, he softly caressed her round plump golden-brown ass and then slapped it firmly. The shock of the smack making her clench and he slammed into her at the same time. Sunny screamed into the cushion of the couch so loudly that it still pierced his ears.

Something inside him snapped and he hammered into her making her cheeks ripple with the force. The trailer was filled with the sounds of their skin slapping together and their cries of pleasure.

Sunny's thighs started to shake uncontrollably and her inner walls started to quake with the first signs of an impending orgasm. Gabe's scrotum drew up, also ready to explode.

"Come for me." Gabe bent over to growl in her ear.

And with that, her back bowed and his hips pummeled as they climaxed together. Their wails mixed together as they collapsed in a heap on the couch. The perspiration from their exertion combining to make their skin and clothes stick against each other, their labored breathing slowly calming down.

"Oh. My. God! I think I need a cigarette." She paused. "What was that?!" Sunny exhaled loudly.

"I have absolutely no idea, but sex with you has been the best sex of my life!" Gabe exclaimed passionately against her back.

"Really?" She asked shocked, but pleased.

"Yes! And what's crazy is that it's different every time. I have no idea what to expect going in. Pun intended." He chuckled in between kissing her one bare shoulder.

"I concur." She smiled into the couch cushion.

Gabe slowly disentangled himself from Sunny's lifeless limbs. "I'm gonna get in the shower. It's a little shower, but you can join me if you'd like, it'll be tight, but we can fit. And plus, it's just how I like you...up close and personal." She didn't move, so he smacked her ass making her yelp and sit up quickly.

"By the way...I owe you for that ass-slap you gave me earlier!" She glowered at him.

"What?! I was in the moment!" Gabe held up his hands defensively.

"Mmmhmm...Well, you better be glad I liked it." She said quickly switching gears, winking at him.

Gabe already shocked by her confession of liking it a little rough, his mouth dropped open further when he watched Sunny let her skirt fall to the floor as she sauntered towards the bathroom. Stepping out of it without even stopping, then she gracefully pulled her shirt up and over her curves, tossing it to land on top of his head.

"Oh ho! That was a huge mistake lady!" Gabe pulled the shirt with her delicious scent from his face and chased her into the bathroom.

They spent the next twenty minutes getting a little dirtier, up against the wall of the shower, once again their cries of ecstasy amplified by the acoustics between the shower walls. Finally they were satiated enough to just wash each other.

After they were dressed again, Gabe unlocked the door and stepped out of the trailer with Sunny close behind him when cheers, whistles, catcalls and clapping greeted them. Gabe chuckled sheepishly, while Sunny hid behind him with her face buried in his back in mortification. He reached around to grab her arm, struggling to get her from behind his back.

"Come on, we might as well give them what they want and get it over with." Gabe grinned at her.

Understanding dawned on her face and with a pretty blush spreading across her cheeks, she clasped his hand and they both took a deep bow. The roar of the cast and crew grew louder with their approval.

"I need a beer." Sunny grumbled to herself, shaking her head.

Gabe laughed and pulled her over to the food truck to get her what she wanted. She deserved it after that show.

~~~

Sunny finished her beer tossed it in the garbage, then walked back to Gabe's trailer to grab some bottles of water for Gabe, Kyle and a few others. *Ha! I'm a gofer on a movie set...awesome!*

She passed a crew member and he gave her a knowing smile. Sunny blushed all the way to her roots. Everyone had been really cool about what Sunny was now calling the 'incident', just a little harmless teasing here and there. She still couldn't believe that she had thrown all her inhibitions right out the window with such abandon. *I'm such a slut!* But that's what Gabe did to her. He made the world disappear around her, as if nothing else mattered but them. And he made her feel comfortable being herself, with her sensuality.

In the trailer she grabbed an armful of bottled water, and then headed back out. Someone standing behind the trailer door as it swung closed startled Sunny so badly that she dropped half the bottles. She squatted down to pick them up.

"I'm sorry I didn't mean to scare you."

Sunny looked up to see Josiah standing over her. He reached down to grab the few bottles that had rolled away from her.

"Oh hey, Josiah. It's okay, I just wasn't expecting anyone to be standing there." Sunny breathed deeply, trying to calm her pounding heart.

Standing up, she finally got a good look at his face. Both of his eyes were black and purple and an angry cut ran across the bridge of his once straight nose.

"Oh my God, Josiah! What happened to your face?!" Sunny asked in shock.

"Maybe you should ask your boyfriend that. I can't believe he didn't tell you." Josiah said in a bitter tone.

"He didn't tell me anything. He *hit* you?!" Sunny was incredulous.

"Yep. A real winner you've got there." Josiah sneered.

Sunny stood awkwardly not knowing what to say. She wanted to defend Gabe, but had no idea what happened between them.

"So…that was a nice little performance you gave earlier." Josiah stepped into her personal space, making her uncomfortable and nervous.

"Um…I don't think that's really any of your business." Sunny tried to step back, but was trapped by the trailer.

"Well sweetheart, you made it everyone's business."

He moved towards her again until they were toe to toe, his face bent only inches from hers. He raised his hand and traced his index finger down the side of her face and tried to caress her bottom lip. She turned her head away and tried to slide out from under him, but he caged her in with his arms and pressed his body against her. She could feel his erection. She wanted to scream and puke at the same time. And she realized in that moment that whatever the reason was that Gabe broke Josiah's face, it was justified.

"When he gets tired of you…and he will, you should give me a call. I've never had black pussy before, but from what I heard earlier, I wouldn't mind getting a taste." Josiah said as he rubbed his erection against her.

"Josiah, you really need to back the fuck off!" Sunny yelled into his face.

One moment he was in her personal space and the next he was gone. Sunny saw a flash of Gabe's enraged face. And then all hell broke loose. The crew ran towards them as Gabe had Josiah shoved up against the trailer, his hands around Josiah's throat, crushing his trachea.

"I warned you to stay the fuck away from her. And you put your fucking hands on her?!" Josiah just gurgled in response. "I'll fucking kill you, you piece of shit!" Gabe's face was molten red and shook with fury.

Several men were on Gabe, trying to pry him off Josiah. But nothing they tried could get him off, his rage giving him the strength of ten men. Tears that she couldn't stop started to fall down Sunny's cheeks. First, from the fear of what Josiah was capable of doing to her and no one being there to stop him. And second, from the fear of what would happen to Gabe if he killed this man.

The latter spurred her into action. Stepping close to Gabe, she gently placed her hand on his arm. "Gabriel stop. You're killing him. Baby, please." She pleaded with him softly, but firmly.

Finally her calm voice was able to do what none of the strong men could. Gabe released Josiah's throat and the man fell to the ground gasping for air. Gabe stood over him with fists clenched, chest rising and falling harshly and jaw flexing. Sunny grabbed his arms forcing him to turn and look at her. His eyes looked so distant and bleak.

"Gabriel, it's okay. He didn't hurt me." Sunny tried to get through to him.

"He fucking put his hands on you." Gabe growled.

She cupped his face in her hands, "Baby I'm fine. He's a dick, but you shouldn't have to go to jail because of him. He's not worth it."

Kyle came over to them, a grim look on his face. "Sunny what exactly happened?"

She looked at Gabe not wanting to piss him off all over again.

"Go ahead. Tell him, I've got it under control now." Gabe reassured her.

Sunny explained exactly what Josiah had said and did. As she told the story, Gabe's jaw was clenched so tight, she thought he'd crack it.

"I've had enough of his bullshit. I'm done." Kyle said fuming. He walked over to where Josiah was being looked at by the set paramedic. "Josiah, you're done. You're off the movie. I'd rather deal with the hassle of bringing in someone else to replace you, than to continue to deal with your shit."

"What?! That's bullshit!" Josiah exclaimed gravelly, his throat obviously still sore.

"You fucking heard me! And don't even think about pressing charges against Gabe or I'll have Sunny file a sexual harassment suit against you so fast your head will spin. Now get off my set." Kyle said with deadly finality.

Josiah glared at Gabe and gave Sunny an evil calculating look that made her shutter with dread. He stormed off swiping scripts, cups of coffee and other various items off a table as he passed it. Sunny prayed she'd never have to cross paths with him again.

~~~

When Gabe had rounded the corner, checking to see what was taking Sunny so long, never in a million years had he expected to see what was going on in front of him. At first when he'd seen Josiah pressing Sunny up against the trailer, running a finger down her face, he'd stopped in his tracks instantly thinking that Sunny didn't want him anymore. Never having been loved before her, it was easy for him to doubt that it would last.

But then Gabe had seen Josiah rub himself against Sunny and her resounding yell to back off, her voice sounding angry yet shaky with fear. In that moment when he realized that the attention was unwanted, Gabe's world went red. He really couldn't even explain to anyone if they asked, what had happened between that moment of seeing red and the moment when he'd heard Sunny calmly telling him to stop. If it hadn't been for her soothing voice, Gabe had no doubt that he'd have killed Josiah.

After Josiah stormed off, he took Sunny into the trailer so she could have a break from the crazy commotion on the set. Gabe's hands started to shake as he came down from the adrenaline rush. She turned into him, pressing her face into his chest and wrapping her arms around his waist. He tried to hold onto her to control the tremors, but they started in his hands and spread through him, until his whole body was shaking.

"Aw baby, you're shaking. Here, come sit with me." Sunny led him to the couch, where they'd just had incredible sex only about an hour ago.

"It's nothing. Just coming down from the adrenaline rush. I'm sorry, Sunny. I didn't mean to lose it like that. I'm not even sure what happened, I just saw red." Gabe looked down at the floor.

"What did he do before, to make you punch him in the face?" Sunny asked curiously.

"He just said some insulting things about you, along the lines of what he said to you earlier. I warned him not to go near you again, but it's as if he has some kind of vendetta against us or something." Gabe looked honestly perplexed and Sunny didn't feel any better.

"It's not just him either. My friends at work read the tabloids and watched that video, and now they won't leave me alone about it. I yelled at one of them, and now I'm some social pariah. And just like Josiah, one of them said that you'd get tired of me eventually. And the sad part is that I believe them." Sunny's eyes welled with tears again.

"God Sunny, they...*you* couldn't be more wrong! And I have absolutely no idea what else I can do or say to make you understand that there isn't or ever will be anyone else for me...ever." Gabe said vehemently, grabbing her shoulders to turn her to face him. "Do you understand me...*no one*?! I have never loved anyone. And no one has loved me. Can you imagine twenty years of never being loved by a family, friends or the opposite sex? Rarely ever getting a hug or any sign of affection? And then spending eighteen years in the spotlight, where everyone claims to love you, but is only looking to get something out of you? The light and love you give me freely, without wanting anything in return, slays me! And I keep waiting for the bottom to fall right out from under me. Because there is no way that this beautiful extraordinary woman could love me as much as I love her." His throat was thick with emotion.

"But I do." Tears slowly running down her cheeks, Sunny crawled onto his lap, resting her knees on either side of his hips. "Just as hard as it is for you to believe, the same goes for me. I love you to distraction. And you've ruined me for anyone else."

Gabe clutched her face in his hands. He kissed every inch of her face finally stopping at her lips. He cherished her mouth, licking and biting and plunging his tongue into its deep recesses. She quickly unfastened his pants and without hesitation lifted her skirt and slid down his impressive length. The move made easier by the lack of panties, she'd never put back on.

They tugged and pulled urgently at each other's shirts until their bare chests made contact, their bottoms still on but out of the way just enough for their intimate connection. Gabe kissed a damp trail down her jaw, neck and chest, until he finally latched onto her breast. He sucked the tender peak into his mouth swirling his tongue around her areola and puckered nipple. Sunny sighed and rested her cheek on top of his soft hair, their hips rocking together unhurriedly.

After showing her other breast the same loving attention, Gabe moved back up to her lips. This time around, their mouths caught the moans and pants from their lovemaking. As his cock continued thrusting into her, his tongue followed the exact rhythm, plunging in at the same time. The simultaneous stimulation of the walls of her mouth and vagina heightened her arousal. The intense waves of their mutual climax rose and washed over them, as his shaft pumped his seed into her and her pussy clenched and drenched him with her wetness. Their arms wrapped around one another, the embrace so tight they couldn't tell whose heartbeat was whose. Gabe's forehead pressed against Sunny's, their breaths mingled in the space between their mouths.

They sat, still connected intimately at the hips, peering into the other's eyes. Warm honey and brilliant blue, both conveying all the love they felt with no words.

Chapter 14

Sunny didn't see Gabe for the two days prior to the movie premiere Friday night. And they were two days of hell.

Not just because she hadn't seen him and she craved being near him every moment of the day, but because her life was spiraling quickly out of her control. Every day she was bombarded with more and more paparazzi that she couldn't even go to the grocery store in her sweats anymore, not unless she wanted her big sweatpants-clad-ass splashed on the front cover of some gossip rag.

Her privacy had become a thing of the past. When she left her apartment for any reason at any time, they were waiting outside her apartment, flashes blinding her and questions thrown at her.

"Are you and Gabriel Wolf dating?"

"Is it serious?"

"Is Gabriel good in bed?"

"Does he have a big package?"

"Are you an aspiring actress and he's helping your career?"

"Are you pregnant with Wolf's baby?"

"Has he proposed yet?"

"What date is the wedding set for?"

"Does Gabriel have any weird birthmarks?"

"Is he kinky in bed?"

"Did he really ask you to go on a diet before he'd marry you?"

"Is Gabriel circumcised?"

"Has Wolf always liked black women?"

Sunny had no idea where they got this shit from. Did they just make stuff up to move magazines off the shelves or did they have a source that was feeding them this garbage? *'Is Gabriel circumcised?!?' Really?!* The questions couldn't have been more invasive if they tried. And the race thing was throwing her for a loop too. She and Gabe had never even brought it up. It never even crossed their minds. They loved each other regardless of color. He was just Gabe. And she was just Sunny.

And these guys didn't just stalk her at home, they also followed her to work. Most of them waited outside for her shift to be over. But there were those who were bolder and came inside and asked her co-workers questions about her. So now she had to worry that she was going to lose her job because the cameramen were intimidating the customers and the company was losing sales. Or that the property management of her apartment building would kick her out because of tenant complaints. She had already received warnings from both after only a few days of this.

So the main reason she hadn't seen Gabe was because she'd refused to leave her apartment any more than she needed to. Not even for lunch with him and the awesome cast and crew she had come to love. And if he so much as showed up at her apartment, it would be a feeding frenzy of paparazzi, like sharks happening upon a school of fish.

All of the scrutiny and self-imposed isolation of the past two days already had Sunny going into a state of depression. *How am I going to keep this up?*

Gabe wanting no argument, had setup a spa day for Sunny. So that afternoon before the premiere, Sunny found the pampering she was receiving at the posh spa a welcome relief. Especially since not one single person had asked her about Gabe. *He must have paid them extra to shut the hell up.*

She had been fed, dipped, exfoliated, waxed, massaged, buffed and now moisturized. It felt great to not have to do it herself for once. And after all that, he had even sent over a makeup artist and hair stylist to give her a fresh look. She had drawn the line though at having a stylist come with different designer clothes to choose from. She had been afraid that any of the clothes they'd have brought wouldn't fit her anyway and she didn't want to be humiliated. But she had told Gabe that she was wearing her favorite black and white polka dot dress with the hot pink accessories that she had worn the night he came to see her sing. He said that he thought the ensemble was perfect for the evening, and let her have her way in that one thing.

So after it was all said and done; her skin had a healthy glow, her makeup was flawless and natural, and her curly hair was somehow manipulated into soft sensual waves that framed her face, shoulders and back. She felt like a different person, ready to make her debut and to take on the critics. *Yeah right!* But it was nice to dream.

Gabe was meeting her at the spa to take her straight to the famous *Chinese Theater* in Hollywood. Sunny fidgeted with her overnight bag as a sleek black limo pulled up outside the doors of the spa. She had to catch her breath as Gabe got out of the limo. He was dressed in relaxed fit, dark-washed jeans and all white leather *K-Swiss* shoes on bottom. And up top he had on a white button up shirt with the top buttons undone and over it a white tuxedo jacket with black lapels and black detailing on the pockets, with a black and white polka dot handkerchief in the top pocket that matched her dress. The casual on bottom and dressy on top, blended together perfectly to give that 'bad boy on his best behavior' look. *Lord have mercy! I wonder if I can molest him in the back of the limo without ruining our clothes.*

~~~

Even though Gabe had seen her in the outfit before, Sunny took his breath away. It looked like his idea to give her a relaxing spa day had paid off. She looked composed and at ease…and stunning. Her skin had an extra radiant glow, a bronzed shimmer. Her makeup was perfection. Her hair was in long shiny waves, softly highlighting her face. And just like the previous time he'd seen her in it, the dress was sexy yet classy and the 'fuck me' heels, taunted him as usual. *One of these days when she's tired of wearing those, I'm going to display them in a glass case in my living room…with a spotlight.*

"Jesus, Sunny! Once again you leave me speechless. I couldn't be more proud to have you on my arm tonight." He said earnestly, kissing her lightly on her glossy lips. She blushed prettily.

"Gabe, you look incredible. And I love this!" She said fingering the kerchief in his jacket pocket.

"I thought it would be cool to find a way to match you without being cheesy." He smiled bashfully.

"Well you succeeded. You know, for someone who's never had a relationship before, you're awfully romantic. More so than guys who've had plenty." Sunny laid her hand over his heart.

"I don't know. I just try to think of the things that you'd like and I do them. If that makes me romantic, then so be it." He shrugged, trying to be nonchalant about it.

Gabe grabbed her overnight bag from her and escorted her to the limo. She was finally staying the night at his house. And he couldn't wait to show her his home. He was planning to broach the subject of her moving in with him and quitting her job later tonight. He knew it was a little soon, but he didn't like her being alone and dealing with the paparazzi. And her job sucked anyway. If she quit, she could work full time on her screenplays.

Once they were settled in the limo and were on their way, Gabe pulled her into his side. He kissed the top of her hair, restraining himself, not wanting to ruin her appearance.

"Are you ready to be introduced to the world?" Gabe whispered against her hair.

"Not since you put it that way!" Sunny exclaimed.

"Don't worry you'll do fine. I have every faith in you to win them over with your heart…your charm. You'll have them wrapped around your pinky in no time." He kissed her temple.

"One could only hope." She said quietly.

~~~

As the limo pulled up in front of the theater, Sunny's heart practically beat out of her chest. There were people and lights everywhere. Cameras were already flashing and the limo door hadn't even opened yet. And there was a crush of fans screaming at the top of their lungs.

Sunny's chest started to rise and fall rapidly, her breaths shallow. Her vision was starting to blur and sounds became fuzzy.

"Sunny? Baby, breathe!" Sunny tried to focus on Gabe's worried face.

"I think I'm having an anxiety attack!" Sunny breathed in and out.

"I'll be next to you the whole time. I've got you, Sweet Girl." Gabe soothed.

"Okay…okay. Let's go before I lose my nerve." Sunny took one last deep fortifying breath.

Gabe opened the door and stepped out. The roar of the crowd rose to an unbelievable frenzy and the flashes from the cameras tripled in frequency, when they realized it was him. *Jesus! If I was epileptic, I'd already be having a seizure.*

Gabe turned, reached into the limo and held his hand out to her. It seemed as if the world and Sunny held their breaths, the former waiting to see who he was with and the latter waiting to see how she'd be received.

Taking his hand, Gabe helped Sunny out the limo. Sunny stepped out, and the paparazzi converged on them, their cameras shoved in her face. She decided to go to her happy place starring *Gabe & Sunny's Greatest Moments* and focused on his confident smiling face, instead of the blinding flashes. Her smile grew brilliant thinking about the island and his trailer.

Leading her forward onto the red carpet, Gabe entwined his fingers with hers. Leaning in to whisper in her ear, "You're doing great, baby. Are you imagining everyone in their underwear, because you have this happy faraway look on your face?" Sunny chuckled at his joke.

"Nope. I'm remembering hot movie trailer monkey sex."
Sunny smiled at him innocently.

Not having expected her to say that, Gabe burst out laughing.
Sunny just giggled.

"You make me so happy. Do you know that?" Gabe kissed
her temple and the camera flashes increased, if that were even
possible.

"Ditto." She said as they walked over to the section of the
red carpet with the poster for the movie as the backdrop. Gabe
shaking hands and high-fiving fans as they passed.

They stopped at the section where the stars of the movie
would stand to get their pictures taken and have short interviews
about the movie and who they were wearing. Getting out of the
limo was the first big moment, now this would be the second but
most important.

All of the entertainment news shows were there and they all
had close to the same line of questioning.

"So Gabe, who's the lovely lady?"

"This is my girlfriend, Sunny."

"Does she have a last name?"

"Yep."

"What is it?"

"Day."

It took everything that Sunny had not to burst into hysterics
at that one.

"You've been spotted together several times this past week.
Is it serious?"

"It depends on what you consider serious? Are we getting
married tomorrow? No. Are we in a loving relationship like any
normal couple? Yes."

"Are you an aspiring actress?"

Oh, it's my turn now. They finally directed the question to
her.

"No, I'm not."

"She's a very talented screen writer."

Sunny raised an eyebrow at Gabe, to let him know she didn't

like him telling the media that piece of information.

"Oh! What kind of screenplays do you right? Romance? Comedy?"

"Porn."

Sunny said this with a straight face, but unfortunately she was unable to hold it because Gabe choked and then doubled over with big guffaws of laughter. She tried to rub and pat him on the back, but was laughing so hard she didn't accomplish much, except smacking him too hard, which only made them laugh harder. Unable to even talk, they walked away giggling, leaving the last reporter speechless.

Just inside the entrance to the theater, Gabe stopped and kissed her soundly on the lips, not caring who captured the moment.

"You were phenomenal! I've never had so much fun at a red carpet event. But you know you're going to pay for that porn comment. Now they'll be saying you're a pornstar." Gabe smiled at her unconcerned.

"Hey, I was just trying to take my queue from you, mister...Sunny Day!? Do you know how hard it was not to bust out laughing when you said that?!"

"Well I just wanted to keep your real name a secret for as long as possible. They'll figure it out eventually, but I wasn't going to be the one to say it, just so they can go digging into your background." Gabe explained.

"Oh Lord! Well thank God that they'll only find that I was a bookworm and a prude." Sunny rolled her eyes exasperated.

"A prude, huh? Well I think I've officially taken care of that. You're a beast in bed now!" Gabe grinned down at her devilishly.

Gabe stepped closer to her, caressing the bare skin of her back, from the easy access of the keyhole cutout of her dress.

"Gabe..." Sunny whispered breathlessly.

"Hi Gabe, who's your friend?" A voice interrupted their moment.

Sunny and Gabe turned to see it was Sophia Morales, his drop-dead gorgeous co-star for the movie that was premiering tonight. Sunny had watched several movies with the stunning Latin brunette. Sunny felt as attractive as a dumpy old toad, finally seeing the actress in person. She was all tall willowy curves, as opposed to Sunny's short compact large ones.

"Hey Sophia, this is my girlfriend, Sunny", Gabe turned to look at Sunny. "Sunny this is my co-star, Sophia Morales."

The women shook hands. Sophia's a little limper than Sunny's. Sunny wasn't sure if she always shook hands like a limp dick or if it was just because she didn't want to touch Sunny.

"It's really nice to meet you." Sunny said politely, always falling back on the manners that were instilled in her.

"Likewise, I'm sure." Sophia said insincerely.

Sunny watched as the two actors conversed. Sophia was just a little too touchy feely for Sunny's tastes. The gestures too familiar, like they had been intimate. Maybe it was because she was his love interest in the movie. Sunny figured you'd have to become somewhat close to a person you were swapping spit with over and over, even if there was a room full of film crew members.

Though that didn't mean *she* had to like it. So when an opening in the conversation presented itself, Sunny excused herself to the ladies' room.

~~~

Gabe leaned against the wall outside of the women's restroom, waiting for Sunny. He had also excused himself from Sophia, shortly after Sunny had walked away.

He didn't like leaving Sunny for that long, and plus he felt kind of uncomfortable with the way Sophia kept touching him. They had had a brief and passionless fling, during the filming of Clutch. Well, to be fair it felt more passionate at the time, but after sex with Sunny, all the sex he'd had in the past was overshadowed in her wake.

So he removed himself from the awkward situation, to find Sunny. As she walked out of the bathroom, she was again looking down to check to make sure there was no tissue stuck to her shoe. Gabe's heart nearly burst with the love he felt for this woman, being hit with the blast of déjà vu. The first night they met seemed like a thousand years ago. He knew the moment he'd laid eyes on her, that she'd change his life forever.

"Well isn't this a familiar sight!" Sunny exclaimed as she walked towards him, bringing him back to the present.

"Unfortunately for me, you didn't accidentally run that lush body into me this time." Gabe grinned down at her.

"*Luckily* for you, I don't have to do it by accident anymore." She said slyly as she purposefully brought her body alongside his, brushing her soft curves against him.

"Oh, you play dirty." He discreetly rubbed his semi-hard erection against her hip. "You'll pay for that later. Now let's go take our seats before the movie starts without us."

Gabe led Sunny into the auditorium and they took their seats in the very middle of the theater. Gabe greeted and shook the hands of other celebrities and film crew that sat around them. He continued to introduce Sunny as his girlfriend. He loved saying it, and apparently she did too, if the flush on her face every time he said it, was any indication.

The audience quieted down as the lights turned low and the screen lit up. For the first time since his first major role in a movie, Gabe was nervous. He was worried whether Sunny would like the film and sitting next to her trying to read her every reaction was going to drive him nuts. Plus, there was the fact that he and Sophia had a pretty steamy love scene in the movie, and he had no idea how Sunny would take it.

So with that, he took his clammy hand and grabbed Sunny's equally sweaty hand, and gave it a fortifying squeeze.

~~~

The movie Clutch was a high-octane thrill-ride, as the tagline on the billboard had promised. And Sunny had to agree. It was a really fun movie to watch. It had gotten her adrenaline pumping, watching Gabe as a renegade cop, who was chasing down the bad guys that had killed his fiancée, all over town in a souped-up *Dodge Challenger*.

During the movie though, Gabe seemed more focused on her reactions than the movie itself. She could tell that he was really nervous, and she smiled to herself over how sweet it was that he cared about her response to the movie.

Even during the love scene between Gabe and Sophia who played his fiancée, his palm got sweatier and he had her hand in a death grip, and worried her knuckles with his thumb. She probably would've been more upset about the scene, if it wasn't for the fact that he was so obviously worried about her reaction to it. It still wasn't easy to watch, but his need for her to be okay with it, put her at ease, knowing she was who he wanted.

When the movie ended, the audience full of Gabe's peers, started clapping heartily, along with Sunny.

"That was fantastic, Gabe!" Sunny looked over at his anxious face.

"Really?" He said doubtfully.

"Definitely! It was fun and fast…and a lot of shit got blown up. What else could you ask for?" She gave him a sassy smile.

"I adore you." Gabe chuckled as he nuzzled the side of her face.

"I know." She laughed and kissed him softly on his firm full lips.

"Do you want to go to the after party?" Gabe asked.

"Hmm…I'd rather be at home alone with you, but I know you should make an appearance."

Gabe found her use of the phrase 'at home' encouraging for the conversation he planned to have later. "Okay, but only for a little while. I want to get you alone too, so that I can ravish that delectable body I know is under that sexy dress." He caressed a finger down her neck, raising goosebumps on her bronzed skin. "With my face buried in my favorite place…between your pretty thighs."

"And…great. My panties are now ruined. Do you know how

uncomfortable it is to walk around with wet chaffing panties?"
Sunny gave him a wicked knowing look.

"I figure just as uncomfortable as it is to walk around with a
restricting boner, like the one you just gave me, with the image of
soaking wet panties." Gabe scowled at her.

"Hey, don't play in the kitchen, if you can't stand the heat."
She winked at him, got up and started heading towards the exit
without him, swaying her hips a little extra to taunt him further.

Gabe got up and stalked her out of the theater.

~~~

The after party was being held on the rooftop bar of the *W*
hotel. Gabe helped Sunny out of the limo and walked her into the
hotel lobby. It had an ultra-modern elegance to it that impressed
Sunny.

In the elevator, they piled in with some of Hollywood's
finest. Two weeks ago Sunny would've been star-struck by all of
the celebrities, but now all she wanted to do was molest Gabe in
the corner. They were pressed into the back of the elevator and
Sunny rubbed her ass imperceptibly across his groin area. To
everyone around them, she was just shifting naturally, but she
knew Gabe wasn't fooled, if his quickly thickening erection was
any indication. Sunny was definitely getting the hang of this
whole seductress thing. She smiled to herself as they made their
way out of the elevator onto the rooftop lounge.

It was decorated in red couches and lounge chairs, with
accents of white in the pillows and billowy cabanas. There was
also a pool and full bar. Sunny was gapping in awe at all of the
high-class decadence.

"Wow! This place is amazing, Gabe." Sunny couldn't focus
on much for too long, because Gabe started pulling her in the
direction of the cabanas.

He nodded his recognition to many of the people he knew,
but didn't stop to speak, dragging Sunny behind him. He pulled
her into a private alcove next to the last cabana, the white canopy

hiding them from the crowd.

Gabe slid his hands up Sunny's thigh, under her dress. "This is for trying to torment me earlier in the theater and elevator." He whispered in her ear.

And that's when she heard and felt the rip of her panties. Gabe's eyes were on fire as he stared down at her while destroying the undergarment. He brought the torn hot pink boy-shorts up to her face. She could smell her arousal on them.

"Open your mouth." Gabe commanded.

She obeyed, and he gently pushed the fabric into her mouth.

"This is so no one can hear you scream." His deep blue eyes were serious and piercing, as her nether regions quivered at his words.

Sunny's eyes widen and nose flared as she moaned against the panties in her mouth. Gabe dropped to his knees, brought one of her legs up to drape over his shoulder and dipped his head under her dress.

Without a moment's hesitation, his mouth was on her wet silt. She automatically bucked against his mouth, having no control over her body. She panted into the panties as they muffled her sounds. Gabe licked and sucked with his lips and tongue, while he slid in and out hitting her g-spot with his middle and index fingers. Sunny thighs started to shake with the unrelenting onslaught of pleasure he was giving her. She grunted and groaned as she pumped her hips onto his hand and mouth. Her whole body started to tingle and tense, and then his fingers hit her g-spot at the same time as his talented tongue flicked up on her clit. And she erupted. She came so hard that her juices literally squirted onto her thighs and his awaiting mouth and chin.

Her whole body was ravaged by violent tremors and her legs were so shaky that she started to fall. But Gabe was there to grasp her hips and steady her before she landed on the ground.

Gabe swept up some of the fluid that was on her inner thighs with his fingers, and looking up at her, he brought his fingers up to his mouth to suck on the tips. "That was new." He said thoughtfully.

Sunny had no time to be embarrassed by the liquid that had gushed all over her and Gabe's face. Gabe had quickly undone his pants, releasing his hard shaft. In his stooped position, he wrapped his arms behind her thighs with his hands resting on her ass cheeks, and then stood up, lifting her up in midair, with her legs spread wide and draped over his arms at the knees. And with no warning or preparation he forcefully thrust into her, all the way to the hilt, hitting the top of her womb so hard that she instantly came again. She cried into the panties and convulsed around his cock. He moaned softly in the back of his throat as he rested his head against her shoulder. He gained leverage when he held her up against the wall and held onto her ass with a bruising grip, and started to pound into her pussy ceaselessly.

The orgasm that she was already in the throes of, rolled into another, and then another as he slammed into her nonstop. Tears started streaming down her face with the torture of the multiple climaxes without a break in between. There was nothing that she could do to stop him. She couldn't move her legs with the position they were in. And she refused to remove the panties from her mouth to beg him to stop or she'd scream the place down and everyone would come running. So she started beating on his shoulders and back, finally grabbing his hair, and with a pull that probably ripped out some of his hairs, forced Gabe to look at her so he could see her helpless agony.

The instant he looked into her pleading eyes, she felt his cock jerk and flood her insides with his release as he stifled the groan that rumbled in his chest. Sunny's pussy continued to spasm around him as he softened. Her body was racked with shudders. He must have known that putting her down on her feet would be a bad idea. So he walked her over to the bed inside the private cabana and laid her down. He slid out of her weeping and abused labia, and disappeared. She didn't move, couldn't move. Not even to pull the panties from her mouth. She just laid there, eyes closed and chest heaving.

She then felt Gabe's presence again, could smell his scent of woodsy cologne and sex. Then she felt a warm wet cloth against the bruised flesh at the juncture her thighs, causing her body to flinch at the soreness. Gabe cleaned her up and then removed the underwear from her slack lips. *What, was he so important that he had people with warm damp towels waiting around the corner?*

"I'm so sorry, Sunny. I didn't mean to get so carried away. It's just that I haven't seen you in a couple of days, you look so beautiful and the constant fear of my life being too much for you, kinda made me lose it. I can't get enough of you and want to be as close to you as possible." Sunny could hear the concern in his voice, and could only assume his face probably matched the emotion since she still hadn't opened her eyes yet.

Sunny just turned and curled up on her side, not able to even express, let alone comprehend what she was feeling. The sex had been intense, wonderful, but scary. *Like he went all* Christian Grey *on my ass. Maybe we need a safeword.*

"I'll just give you some time to recuperate. I left you something to drink on the table. I love you." Gabe kissed her temple and left the cabana. *I love you, too.*

~~~

When Sunny felt like she was composed enough, she finally extricated herself from the bed of the cabana. She grabbed the glass of water that Gabe had left for her, and chugged it down, needing something stronger. Then straightening her dress and smoothing down her hair, hoping that she looked somewhat presentable and not like she'd been fucked within an inch of her life, she walked out of the cabana and over to the bar. She ordered a beer from the bartender, and when she had her drink, she went in search of Gabe.

She found him sitting on the couches with a couple of men in deep discussion.

"I'll send it over to you by courier tomorrow." Gabe was saying to one of the men. Gabe looked up when she came to stand next to him. He stood and kissed her forehead, "Hey Sweet Girl, are you okay?" He said quietly, his voice nervous.

"Yeah, I'm good. No worries." She wrapped an arm around his waist and squeezed, letting him know that she wasn't upset with him.

He released the breath that he had been holding and his entire body relaxed. He had really been tearing himself up about what happened.

"Okay, good. Are you ready to go?" He smiled tentatively at her.

"Yeah. I'm getting pretty tired." Sunny said stifling a yawn that came out of nowhere.

"Alright." He chuckled.

He quickly introduced her to the director and two producers that he had been sitting with, made their excuses, and then headed to the elevators.

Back inside the limo, Gabe wasted no time pulling Sunny onto his lap. He nuzzled his face in her hair, breathing deeply.

"Are you sure you're okay? You're not mad at me?"

"Gabe, sweetie. What am I gonna say? That I'm mad at you for giving me so many multiple orgasms that I nearly passed out? Yes, it was a little intense and scary, but stop beating yourself up about it. A girl should be so lucky." Sunny cupped the side of his face, staring into his eyes lovingly.

"So what you're saying is, I'm the most amazing lover you've ever known?" Gabe joked, trying to lighten the mood.

"Oh Lord. Well that goes without saying. You're such a dork." Sunny giggled and held him tight.

"But I'm your dork." He finally relaxed fully, now that he knew the crisis was averted.

By the time they got to his house, Sunny had drifted off to sleep in his arms. Light kisses all over her face woke her up. She gave Gabe a sleepy smile.

"We're here, Sweet Girl."

"Alright…alright. I'm up."

They got out of the limo and Gabe guided her over to a huge privacy wall and gate. She could only see part of the roof of the house from outside. No wonder he lived here, the seclusion from the press was worth whatever the price was, as far as she was concerned. She had been dealing with it for only two weeks and she thought she was going insane.

Gabe punched in a code on the keypad, and the gate started to swing open. Sunny gasped at the vision in front of her. The house appeared to blend perfectly with the mountain behind it. It had the feel of a Spanish villa; stucco, large stones, and a tiled roof. There was a sandstone path that wove its way through the grass to the front door. The lights along the path and from inside the house gave a soft, warm, and welcoming glow.

"Some of the lighting is controlled by the security system. At night when I use the gate opener in one of my vehicles or I punch in the code, the lights on the path and a select few inside, turn on." Gabe explained.

"I can't even explain how beautiful I think your home is. And I haven't even seen the inside yet." Sunny said with her mouth hanging open and her eyes wide with wonder.

"I'm glad you like it. Come on, I'll show you the inside."

Gabe unlocked and opened the door for Sunny. She walked into the most beautiful house she'd ever seen. It was all cream walls, cherry wood ceilings with I-beams, gray and tan stone details in the fireplaces and entryway, and reddish tan Spanish tile on the floor. The house itself was very 'old world', but his furnishings were more modern with 'old world' accents here and there. And everything was in warm earth tones.

And the backyard was paradise. He had the trees and plant life balanced to flow with the plants of the mountain. A grassy section was on the side and curved around the house, a space to play yard games at barbeques or to set up a playhouse for kids. The stone details inside the house were found outside as well, some small and some large to create the pool that looked more like a pond with little waterfalls pouring into it. The recessed lighting produced a seductive yet calming oasis.

For whatever reason she couldn't place, Sunny's eyes blurred with moisture, overwhelmed by emotions. If she looked deeper she knew that she'd find what she felt was peace. As if she had come home. But if she accepted this place as her home and things didn't work out between them, she was afraid that she would never feel at home again...anywhere.

"So what do you think? You haven't said much during your tour." Gabe asked concerned.

"I have no words. That's why I've been so quiet. It's absolutely stunning...perfection." She ended softly.

"You have no idea how happy it makes me that you love it." Gabe breathed in relief. "Here, let's go back inside. You go change into your pajamas, I'll get you a beer and we can relax."

"Okay."

~~~

Sunny padded barefoot out of the bathroom that adjoined the master bedroom. Gabe groaned internally at what she was wearing. After what happened on the rooftop of the hotel, he had promised himself that he wouldn't touch her again tonight, to give her space. And even though she was wearing some seductive blue silk and black lace baby doll nightie that only covered the tops of her beautiful thighs, he still wasn't going to give in. *Nope. No. I'm not gonna do it.*

"Come sit over here. I want to talk to you about something." Gabe led her to the couch he had in front of the large bedroom windows overlooking the backyard. He figured it'd be a safer spot than the bed. *Yeah, right. Like that matters. Couches are our thing.*

"Okay, so what did you want to talk about?" Sunny asked nervously as she took the glass of beer he gave her.

Gabe inhaled deeply and then blew it out quickly. "Okay, don't answer until you've given it some real thought... I want you to move in with me. Make this a home with me, not just a house." He gestured around indicating the house.

Sunny's expressive eyes filled with hope and excitement, and then a second later the emotions were squashed down by a look of doubt.

"I don't know Gabe. It's just so-"

"Soon." Gabe finished for her.

"It's just that my place is perfect for me and the rent is amazing. If things don't work out between us, I'll have no place to live. And more than likely won't find something that cheap again." Sunny tried to rationalize.

"Sunny even if we didn't work out, there is no way in hell that I'd just put you out on the street. I'll take care of you no matter what. And I hate that you have to deal with the paparazzi all by yourself. Your building has no real security. I worry about you all the time." Gabe pleaded his case.

"I know." Sunny looked down at her hands.

"And that's not all." Sunny looked up at him. "I want you to quit your job too. To work on your screenplays. To have the career you were meant to have."

"Gabe! I can't be completely dependent on you! Quit my job...seriously?!" Sunny exclaimed.

"But you won't be dependent on me. You'll have your work. Which I already have an interested party wanting to read one of your scripts. The director I introduced you to before we left the hotel. And Sunny, if you sell just one of your scripts to someone, you'll make more money in that one sale than you would make in a whole year at your job!" Gabe said excitedly, pleading his case.

"It's just such a huge risk." Sunny gulped down her beer and then started to fidget with the empty glass nervously.

"Life is a risk. And you're overthinking everything. Remember...stop thinking and *feel*! And when you're ready, let me know what you decide. But you don't have to do it now. Let's just get some sleep."

He took Sunny's empty glass and set it on the table. Then he led her to the giant king size bed, laid her down, crawled in behind her and pulled her close.

Chapter 15

Sunny woke up the next morning wrapped in a 'man' cocoon. Gabe's arms tightly encircled her and his legs were tangled with hers. She lay still not wanting to wake him, while she thought about all that he'd said the night before. Was she ready to jump?

She felt his arms tighten even more around her, and then she detected a very distinct erection between the cheeks of her backside. She just smiled and rubbed her ass against his thick shaft, offering herself up to him. She knew that he had restrained himself last night after the wild rooftop sex, and she wanted to let him know that it was okay to proceed.

Taking her queue that all was well, he lifted her leg back over his hip. He slowly slid the head of his cock up and down her wet cleft, and then glided himself in from behind. She gasped, arched her back and pushed harder against him.

"Yes, Gabe. I say, yes." Sunny said breathlessly as he thrust into her again.

"What?" He panted.

"Yes, I'll move in with you."

He suddenly flipped her over onto her back. And stared into her eyes, searching to make sure she wasn't messing with him.

"Really? You mean it?" He said trying not to get too excited.

"Yes, really." Sunny rolled her hips up to him to try and get back the connection. But he wasn't biting.

"When?" He looked so hopeful, her heart warmed.

"Soon. I just have to get things settled and give my notices at work and the apartment. Now stop stalling and fuck me already!"

Sunny growled in frustration.

"Yes, ma'am."

Gabe plunged into her depths and they both cried out. As Gabe brought them both to a shattering climax, Sunny felt like everything was right with the world…she was home.

~~~

That feeling of rightness lasted all of two seconds. In the days following the premiere and her debut, Sunny virtually became a hermit. Introducing her to the media only caused their interest in her to peak, not wane, like they had thought.

She was constantly hounded, and the amount of paparazzi had doubled. And someone, (she had a sinking suspicion was one of her co-workers/ex-friends), leaked her real name to the media. And even her cell number. So now, even her phone was ringing off the hook. She couldn't find any peace from the chaos. The press called with more invasive questions that she didn't answer and offers of money to be interviewed by them first, which she turned down. *I need to change my fucking number.*

Sunny gave up on all media outlets too. She stopped watching television and refused to go online. She had tried going on *Facebook* only through her cell app, but even gave up on that when all her friends starting asking questions about her relationship with Gabe.

She had enlisted Alyssa to be her eyes and ears of the media. Alyssa reported back to her on if she was perceived well at the premiere and if there were any other new and/or false rumors buzzing around. Alyssa filtered out the really negative comments that Sunny didn't want to hear.

Alyssa had said that there were some insults here and there, but mostly from haters that liked to leave mean comments on entertainment articles and videos. Sunny knew that was the norm nowadays. People felt that because they were behind a computer screen and not face to face, that it offered them some form of anonymity. Not realizing that they were the cause of permanent pain for many that they insulted. So she had no plans to read that crap, trying to filter out the good from the bad.

Alyssa had told her that though there was some bad, there was a lot of good. Apparently after the videos of them at the premiere were aired, most people loved them as a couple. They said that they were genuine and cute together. And there were a lot of girls that were impressed and inspired by Sunny, to be themselves, and maybe they too would find their own *Gabriel Wolf.*

That was the best part for Sunny, knowing that she was inspiring girls. But all she wanted was her privacy back and to enjoy her life and relationship. She even used some of her sick days to avoid going in to work, to get some peace. *Hell, I'm quitting anyway.*

Sunny's phone rang, and she breathed a sigh of relief when she heard Alyssa's assigned song.

"Yellow." She answered

"Get your butt up here and keep me company! I'm bored. You might not wanna leave the building, but there's no paparazzo up here. So you have no excuse." Alyssa sniffed into the phone self-righteously.

"I'll be up in just a sec." Sunny responded quickly, needing a break from her thoughts.

"Hmm…that was easier than I thought it would be."

"Yeah, yeah. I need the distraction. See you in a minute."

Sunny stayed in her pajamas, grabbed her phone and went upstairs for some girl time. She knocked on Alyssa's door, which opened immediately. She walked in and shut the door as Alyssa skipped over to her couch.

"I just cracked open a bottle of wine, care to join me?" Alyssa held up the bottle with a raised eyebrow.

"I thought you'd never ask." Sunny took the full wine glass Alyssa poured for her.

They spent the evening talking about Alyssa and Brandon's relationship, which had turned into full-blown couple status while Sunny had been developing her own thing with Gabe.

Sunny was flipping through a fashion magazine while Alyssa went online to check for anymore Gabe & Sunny news. *Thank God they haven't combined our names like Bradgelina!*

"You know Alyssa, if all this craziness continues, I think I'll hire you as my PR person." Sunny said jokingly.

"FUCK! Uh…Sunny?" Alyssa shouted the first word, and then whispered the last apprehensively.

"Oh God…what now?" Sunny asked hesitantly.

"Uh…well they're saying that they have an audio sex tape of Gabe…and the girl on it isn't you." She said with a cringe on her face.

"Is there a link to play it?" Sunny said apprehensively.

"Yeah."

"Play it." Sunny said, her heart in her throat.

Alyssa clicked on the link uncertainly. Then she clicked play on the audio, and the apartment was instantly filled with the sounds of passionate love-making. They both listened for a minute and when Sunny started smiling, Alyssa's mouth dropped open in disbelief.

"How could you be smiling?" Alyssa asked, incredulous.

"That's not another woman that's *me*! I don't like that this got out, but the fact that the rumor isn't true makes me happy." Sunny said relieved.

"How do you know it's you?" Alyssa asked skeptically, still not ready to believe.

"First of all, how can you believe the full of shit media and not your best friend? And second, I know it's me because that's what I sound like when I'm having sex with Gabe. They just edited out when he yelled out my name. That was the day when we kind of got carried away in his trailer." Sunny flushed at the memory.

"Oooh…so this is what everyone heard that day?! DAMN!!! You guys are smokin' hot together! Alyssa fanned herself.

"Shut up." Sunny threw a pillow at her friend. "The question is, why would anyone want to lie about who the girl is on the tape? Or better yet, who would even fucking record us!?" Sunny wondered out loud.

"Who knows. Someone is just jealous and wants to ruin your relationship. And I'm sorry I doubted you. I just don't want Mr. Movie Star to hurt you." Alyssa apologized.

"Trust me I don't want that either. But he really seems to love me. He may be famous and a multi-millionaire, but he's had a hard life. And we just kind of click. We'll see where it goes."

~~~

Later, when Sunny was back in her apartment, Beyoncé's *Crazy in Love*, her new assigned ringtone for Gabe started playing.

"Hey, babe." She smiled into the phone.

"Hey, Sweet Girl." His deep voice melting her on the spot.

"So we have a new rumor going around." Sunny said shaking her head, even though he couldn't see it.

"Oh God, what now?" Gabe groaned.

"Well, someone has released our audio sex tape of that day in your trailer. But...they're trying to say it's not me, that it's another woman." Sunny explained.

"Did you listen to it? You don't believe it do you?" Gabe panicked.

"Yes, I listened to it. And no, I don't believe them. But that's mainly because I know that it was me. I know what I sound like when I'm with you. They tried to edit out you yelling my name, but there's no doubt it's me." Sunny soothed.

"Good! Cause you have to know that I haven't been with another woman since I met you?" Gabe said urgently.

"I know Gabe, I trust you."

"Come out for lunch tomorrow, please? I haven't seen you for three days! And that's all the time I am willing to allow." Gabe grumbled into the phone. Sunny could see his pouting face.

"Hmm...I don't know if I want to come to the set though. I'm not really in the mood to socialize."

"We can go wherever you want, baby. Just so long as I can

see you. You should be moved in by now, you know!" Gabe said crossly.

"Right! And how exactly am I going to move, when I can't even get out of my doorway because of all the paparazzi piled in front!" Sunny did some grumbling of her own.

"Oh, don't you even worry your pretty little head about that. I'll hire moving guys. The paparazzi won't even know it's you that's moving. So get that sweet ass moving, before I have to turn into a caveman and resort to the 'clunk and drag' method."

Sunny fell over on her futon, laughing hysterically. "I love you, but you're crazy man!" She used her best Will Farrell in *Old School* impersonation.

"So anyway, what would you like to do for lunch tomorrow?" Gabe asked not giving up on the subject.

"Let's go to *Rock Bottom*. It's right across the street from my place. I'll meet you there." Sunny suggested.

"I can come get you."

"I know that. But the two of us together would cause a media frenzy, and I just don't want that outside of my building. The other tenants are already freaking out." Sunny said, shaking her head in frustration.

"Alright, I'll meet you there." Gabe conceded.

"Okay, go get some sleep Mr. Wolf, you sound exhausted."

"Yes, ma'am. I love you, Madison Stone." Gabe said softly.

"And I love you, Gabe." Sunny sighed before hanging up.

~~~

Sunny threw on some jeans, ballet flats and a pretty coral top that complimented her skin. She wanted to be comfortable, just in case she had to make a quick dash from the cameramen. She had no idea how right she was.

Stepping out of her building, what felt like hundreds of flashes exploded in her face, blinding her. They all converged on her at once, and she realized that not having Gabe meet her was a bad idea. All she could do now was head in the direction she knew *Rock Bottom* should be. If she'd have been thinking rationally, she would've just stepped back inside her apartment and called Gabe to come get her or cancelled all together. But she continued to walk with her head down, while the men jostled her and asked her questions.

"*Do you know who that was on the tape with Gabriel?*"

"*There's a rumor that's saying its Sophia Morales. Is that true?*"

"*Are you devastated that he cheated on you?*"

"*Have you broken up?*"

"*Do you have an open relationship?*"

"*Do you get to watch when he has sex with other women?*"

The questions continued, on and on, overlapping until it all sounded like a jumbled mess, and she couldn't understand any of it. She stopped at the corner of the intersection across from the restaurant. The men in the back were pushing forward to try and get their chance at her, which pushed the men in front onto her.

Sunny raised her hands to her ears and squeezed her eyes shut. "Please, just leave me alone!" She shouted and without thinking stepped into the street to get away from them.

All she saw next was the flash of a silver grill in the sunlight coming at her. She raised her arms to protect her face, and felt a crack of pain, followed by blackness. Before the blackness swallowed her whole, she heard one last thing…the anguished scream of her name. Then her world went black.

~~~

Gabe realized that he had gotten to the restaurant first. He asked the hostess to be seated at a table on the patio facing the street, so that he could watch for Sunny. The hostess and a waitress politely asked for his autograph and a picture with him on their cellphones, before she took him to his table.

By the time he had gotten to the table, Sunny was directly across the street, surrounded by paparazzi. She had a panic stricken look on her face. Gabe's heart started pounding. He went to the railing of the patio and leaped over it with little effort, adrenaline pounding through his veins with the need to help her.

But before he could get to her, he watched in horror as she stepped out into traffic, and right in front of a full-sized pickup truck. The guy in the truck tried to slam on the brakes, but it was too late. Sunny instinctively lifted her arms to protect her face and the truck hit her right arm and body, throwing her back onto the pavement, her head cracking against the asphalt.

Gabe heard himself scream her name, but the sound seemed so detached and faraway that it took him a moment to realize it was him. Traffic stopped instantly, realizing that something was wrong. And he bolted out into the street.

The fucking paparazzi just stood over her, surrounding her limp unconscious frame taking pictures instead of making sure she was okay. Once again, blinding rage filled Gabe and he ran over with fists flying. He smashed his fists into two of the men and crushed three cameras, before they realized they should back off.

Once clear he dropped to his knees in front of Sunny, wanting to touch her, but knowing that if he moved her he'd probably only cause her more damage. So instead he just clenched and unclenched his shaking hands at his sides.

"Someone call 911…NOW!" He screamed into the gathering crowd.

"I already did. Someone is coming." The man that was driving the truck said shakily. "I'm so sorry, man. I didn't mean to hit her."

"I know." Was all Gabe could get out, as he heard the distant sounds of an ambulance siren getting closer.

Gabe felt her neck, trying to check for a pulse. He found it, but it felt faint to him. *Please God, don't let her die.*

Gabe bent over Sunny with his face buried in his hands, while tears ran silently down his face and into his palms. One car accident had altered his life nearly thirty-eight years ago, it couldn't possibly be happening again.

The ambulance pulled up and the paramedics jumped out and

came over with a stretcher and neck brace, making Gabe stand and backup. He stood helpless as they worked on her. Cameras flashed around him from paparazzi and bystanders, but Gabe didn't register any of it. All he could think of was how his life would never be the same if she didn't make it.

Once they had her in the neck brace and on the stretcher, they loaded her into the ambulance. Gabe got in the back without question, not willing to be separated from her.

"Is she okay?" He asked the paramedic that was in the back with them.

"Yeah, for now. She hit her head pretty hard and it looks like she broke her arm. It's hard to tell if anything else is wrong, until we get her to the hospital." The paramedic explained with grave seriousness.

Gabe just nodded, trying to keep it together. When they got to the hospital, they rushed her into the ER, then a doctor working on her told Gabe that they needed to get her to surgery, because she had internal bleeding. For the first time since he was a kid, Gabe began to sob.

When he finally pulled it together, he called Alyssa to tell her what had happened. And then he called Kyle to let him know that he wouldn't be back on the set today.

A short while later Alyssa, and then Kyle with a few other film crew members that adored Sunny, showed up at the hospital to see how she was doing and to give Gabe support.

Gabe could only sit for a few minutes at a time, before he was up and pacing back and forth again. He wanted to scream at every person he saw that passed by in scrubs, to let him know if she was okay. Instead he just kept quiet and scowled at everyone, as he screamed in his head. *What the fuck is taking so long?!*

Finally a doctor in his late forties, in green scrubs with those little booties that covered their feet during surgery, came around the corner. Gabe rushed up to him with Alyssa and Kyle on either side of him, just as anxious as he was to know if Sunny was okay.

"Mr. Wolf, I'm Dr. Victor Stevenson. Ms. Stone is doing well." He smiled at them. They all released the breath they had been holding. "Ms. Stone suffered a broken forearm, concussion and a pretty nasty gash on her head that we had to stitch up. But the worst of it was from a ruptured stomach. We had to go in and sew her up, she's going to be a little sore, but should make a full recovery."

"Oh thank God!" All three said at the same time.

"Can I see her?" Gabe asked.

"She's in Recovery right now, but as soon as she's settled in her room, that should be fine."

"I want her in her own private room. I want her as comfortable as possible. I'll pay for it." Gabe's tone brooked no argument.

"Yes, Mr. Wolf. I'll talk to the nurses and have them set it up."

"Thank you, doctor." Gabe shook the doctor's hand, and then collapsed in a chair, breathing a huge sigh of relief.

About a half an hour later, a nurse gave them the okay to see Sunny. She directed them to the right room and told them Sunny should be awake any moment.

Gabe walked into the hospital room first, his heart stuttered when he saw her little body in the bed, with tubes coming out of her. Her head was partially wrapped in gauze temporarily, in case her stitches bled a little. She had scrapes and bruises on her left arm, hands and face. And her right arm was in a cast, from hand to armpit. Even her beautiful bottom lip was split.

Gabe reached out a shaky hand to gently brush her face. His other hand holding hers and stroking it with his thumb. Alyssa pulled up a chair for him to sit in next to the bed. He sat down and laid his head on the hand he was holding next to her hip, silently crying. *Thank you. Thank you. Thank you.*

He vaguely felt a hand squeeze his shoulder, and then it was completely quiet. He realized that Alyssa and Kyle must have decided to give him some privacy, because the room was empty when he looked up a moment later.

"Wake up whenever you're ready, Sweet Girl. I'll be here. I've got you." Gabe whispered to Sunny.

~ 180 ~

Sunny woke up to the sound of incessant beeping that was driving her nuts. And then pain…excruciating pain. The pain radiated all over her body. But it was mainly concentrated in her head, right arm and stomach. *What the hell*! Sunny's eyes fluttered opened and she groaned from the pain.

The moment she realized she was in a hospital room, memories bum-rushed her; the paparazzi, the chaos, and the flash of a truck. Her heartbeat picked up speed and so did that stupid beeping sound. She looked down as Gabe's head that had been resting on her hand, popped up. His eyes were red-rimmed and his cheeks were wet from tears. He looked distraught. She tried to lift her hand to touch his face, but couldn't find the strength.

"Aw God, Sunny you're awake!" Gabe sounded relieved.

"Yeah." She croaked like she'd swallowed a frog.

"Are you thirsty, baby?" He grabbed the pitcher of water that was sitting on the tray at the foot of the bed, and poured it into a cup with a straw. He brought it to her lips, holding it while she drank.

"Thank you." Her voice sounded only a little better than before. "What happened?"

"Well, the paparazzi freaked you out and you stepped into traffic. A pickup truck hit you. You blocked your face, which is why when the truck hit you, it broke your arm. And it also hit you hard in your mid-section, so it ruptured your stomach. And finally, after it hit you, you fell back and slammed your head on the pavement, which is why you have a stitched up gash on the back of your head and a concussion." Gabe's face looked haggard, his blue eyes troubled and cloudy.

"Dear Lord! I'm a mess!" Sunny groaned.

"Are you in pain?" She gave him a 'look'. "Of course you're in pain. Let me get a nurse. I'm sure they can give you something to make you feel better."

Sunny just nodded and closed her eyes. She heard him leave

and then a few minutes later, she heard the bustling of a nurse, as she came in the room. She checked Sunny's vitals and then administered some liquid pain meds that went straight to Sunny's bloodstream. She felt like she was on Cloud-nine instantly. *Mmm…that's nice.*

Sunny woke up a while later, right before dawn, if the light outside was any indication. Gabe was in a chair, his head lying on the bed next to her hip, his face turned towards her.

He looked so beautiful and relaxed in sleep. Almost like a little boy, with his long lashes spread cross the tops of his cheeks. She softly touched his dark silky hair, he didn't even move. He must have been exhausted.

Now that Sunny's muddled thoughts were a bit clearer, she started to think about the last three weeks. She was completely head over heels in love with Gabe, and apparently he was with her too. Though, being with him had been some of the best times of her life, loving him was obviously detrimental to her health and his as well. He had been a wreck. And evidently, there were people that didn't want them together. She couldn't go on like this, just waiting for the ball to drop.

With the decision made, she needed to talk to Gabe now, before she lost her resolve. So she ran her fingers through his hair, trying to gently wake him up. Her heart pounded with the stress of what she was about to do. He stirred and looked up at her.

"Hey, Sweet Girl. Are you okay? Do you need anything?" His sleepy voice, combined with his pet name for her, nearly undid her.

So with a voice thick with emotion, she began what she needed to say.

"Gabe, I need to talk to you. I…we can't do this anymore." Her eyes filled with tears and he stared at her in disbelief.

"What are you talking about?" He asked warily. "We can't do what anymore?"

"We can't be together. It's just too much. And it's apparent that people don't want us together." The tears spilled over her eyelids onto her cheeks.

"I don't give a fuck what anyone else wants! *I* want you. I *love* you. You mean everything to me." Gabe pleaded.

"Then if that's true, you'll walk away from me. They practically killed me yesterday, Gabe!" The tears were streaming down her face now. Her eyes so blurry, she could barely see his face, which was a good thing since the look of devastation on it would have killed her. "If you love me, you'll let me go." Sunny knew that was a low blow, turning his love against him.

"Sunny, please don't do this!" Gabe started to beg.

"I'm sorry, Gabe. I just can't do this anymore. I can't see you anymore. I want a normal life, and I can't have that with you." Sunny stared down at her hands, unable to look at him.

"Sunny-"

"Please just go." Sunny interrupted.

Gabe slowly stood up, and looked down at her with the most loving expression she had ever seen in her life. She died a little inside in that moment. He leaned over and kissed her forehead softly.

"I will always love you, Sweet Girl." He whispered against her skin.

Then he straightened quickly and walked out of the room and her life. Sunny turned her head into the pillow, her composure fully breaking and she sobbed uncontrollably. This pain far surpassed the physical pain of her injuries from the accident.

Lost in her own sorrow, she missed Gabe glance back into the room, tears coursing down his face unchecked. Then he turned and with head bowed walked away.

###

Sunny and Gabe's story continues in the exciting conclusion, Awe-Struck.

Acknowledgements

I'd like to thank my parents for supporting me, creatively and financially during the process of writing my first novel.

I'd also like to thank my friends and beta-readers/editors Sue and Randi for taking the time out to be the first to read my novel.
Sue thank you for being my biggest writing fan. Since college, you have read my poems and stories and encouraged me to continue writing.
Thank you Randi for taking the time to read Star-Struck and being the first to let me now that you loved my characters and story. And sitting over the phone with me to edit my typos, page by page. You were my second set of eyes. And I know you love my semi-colons!

And thanks to all my other family and friends who encouraged me and rooted for me…you know who you are. I love all of you!

About the Author

Twyla Turner currently resides in Arizona. She was born and raised in Joliet, Illinois, a Midwest girl at heart, though constantly moving from place to place and always thinking of where she wants to go next. Having been an avid romance novel reader since junior high and minoring in Creative Writing, she felt that it was finally time to start combining her love of travel and writing, as well as her life experiences and putting them down on "paper". Which experiences, she'll never tell…well maybe, if you ask nicely.

Other books by Twyla Turner

The Struck Series:
Star-Struck
Awe-Struck

A Damaged Souls Novel:
Scarred
Open Wounds-Coming Soon

THR3E

Cupid's Secrets Anthology: Love in the Wild

Connect with Me

https://twylaturner11.wix.com/novelswithcurves

Follow me:

https://www.facebook.com/twylaturner11

Twitter: @TwylaTurner11

www.ingramcontent.com/pod-product-compliance
Lightning Source LLC
Chambersburg PA
CBHW070916130626
46555CB00001B/153